RACHEL COHN & DAVID LEVITHAN

SAM & ILSA'S LAST HURRAH

ALFRED A. KNOPF
NEW YORK

THIS IS A BORZOI BOOK PUBLISHED BY ALFRED A. KNOPF

Text copyright © 2018 by Rachel Cohn and David Levithan
Jacket photographs © 2018 by Christine Blackburne/
Merge Left Reps, Inc.

Visit us on the Web! GetUnderlined.com

Educators and librarians, for a variety of teaching tools, visit us at
RHTeachersLibrarians.com

Library of Congress Cataloging-in-Publication Data
is available upon request.
ISBN 978-0-399-55384-4 (trade) —
ISBN 978-0-399-55385-1 (lib. bdg.) — ISBN 978-0-399-55386-8 (ebook)

The text of this book is set in 11.5-point Goudy.

Printed in the United States of America
April 2018
10 9 8 7 6 5 4 3 2 1

First Edition

To my Bubbe and my Bebe grandmas
—RC

To Grandma Grace and Grandma Alice
—DL

People need, demand fantasy. I try to help them do this for a little while, to help them forget work and problems and enjoy, vicariously, a folderol of fun, good music and fancy dress. I give them a little recess from the humdrum.

—LIBERACE

INVITATION

WHAT: Recess from the Humdrum! Dinner Party

WHO: Sam & Ilsa

WHEN: May 16, 8 p.m.

WHY: Last dinner party at Czarina's Palais de Rent Control! Sad face!

Also, Liberace's birthday.* Sequin face!

WHERE: Sam & Ilsa's grandma's** (map attached)

WEAR: Garish***

*If you don't know who Liberace is, we don't know how you got invited to this party. But you can ask Mr. Google if you need help.

**Don't worry, Czarina is out of town and will leave us alone for the evening!

***Ask yourself, WWLW: What Would Liberace Wear?

one

ILSA

My brother is way too obsessed with our grandma's sex life.

"I think Czarina has taken a lover," Sam says, holding out his hand to me. "Spatula. Stat." My job is to maximize the chef's surgical efficiency by passing him the gadgets he requests. I hand him the spatula. "That's an egg-turner spatula. The spoon spatula, Ilsa," he says, like it's so obvious. "Observe!"

I look at his bowl, filled with cheese and spinach. Seems like any old spatula could work in that bowl, but if it were up to me, we'd order takeout from Zabar's and not bother with DIY cooking at all. Sam's an amazing cook. But all that work! No, thank you. He gets me for a half hour as *sous-chef*, and the rest of the meal is on him. My job is planning fabulousness, not catering it. *I* should have been the gay man, not my twin brother.

I hand Sam the spoon spatula. "What makes you think Czarina has taken a lover?"

"She's gone to Paris three times in the last six weeks."

"She's a fashion buyer. That's her *job*."

"There's something different about these trips. I feel it. Did you notice how . . . *nice* she seems when she gets back? It's upsetting."

"What are you really upset about? That she's been nice, or that she took Mom and Dad and not you to Paris with her for the weekend?" I love when Czarina goes away and lets us use her apartment. Then I get to be the queen of her castle, and not have to share Sam with her.

"That's the thing! She never takes Mom and Dad anywhere. Says they're bourgeois bores."

"I love 'em, but they kind of are."

"Don't be bitchy."

"Don't ask me to be anything other than who I am."

Sam laughs, then raises an eyebrow at me. "Aren't you just a little concerned? Czarina even said we didn't have to leave her bedroom door locked. Of all the dinner parties she's let us host in her apartment, her one and only strict rule has been"—and here Sam mimics Czarina's gangster-worthy growl—"'no teenage miscreants shall miscreant in my bedroom.'"

"Yeah, that's why she always shows up during dessert, despite saying she was taking a night out to go to the symphony, and even when she's locked away all the liquor. The control freak can't take our word for it that we won't let anyone in her bedroom or break into her booze." I reconsider what I just said, and then amend my statement. "I mean, take *my* word for it. She knows Sam the Saint won't break her rules."

"Not true. Remember the party when #Stantastic wanted to see Czarina's vintage Dior gowns?"

"You texted Czarina and got her permission to go into her closet. That's not rule breaking."

"#Stantastic had a beer!"

I let out a sigh. "Scandal."

What constitutes legit rule breaking? Perhaps that party two years ago when Parker and I jimmied our way into Czarina's brandy collection and then ended the party making out on her bed, with the bedroom door locked so no one else could get in. Best aperitif ever. Miscreants, and proud! Czarina was in Milan, so I knew for a fact she wouldn't be barging in. My parents say I'm too reckless, but even I know not to expose myself to Czarina's in-your-face wrath. I know exactly how that brutal wrath works, because it's the primary trait of hers I inherited. That, and we both look good wearing almost any shape of hat.

I aspire to be more like Czarina in ways other than being wrathful. I'd like to be a heartbreaker, rather than the one left heartbroken. The boss of any situation. Like Czarina, I want to travel the world and have wild affairs, but with the security of a grand Manhattan apartment as home base. (Insert the sounds of my parents' cynical laughter here.) Unlike Czarina, I don't aspire to wear bright-colored caftans and chunky jewelry as my signature look. Aside from dinner parties, I'll be content with the more humdrum look of skinny jeans and extremely cute tight shirts.

Sam counters my sigh with his own. It might be our only twin thing: supportive sighing. "I can't believe this is our last party here. I can't believe she's finally leaving this place."

Where Sam and I live with our parents—a few blocks away, in a bland Manhattan apartment that's, typically, too small, with an office alcove converted to a third bedroom that Sam uses—is the real humdrum. Czarina's abode? Spectacular. Our grandmother lives in a gorgeous apartment in a historic building called the Stanwyck, on the Upper West Side of Manhattan. It's a huge two-bedroom apartment with a dining room and a study big enough for Sam's piano, and views of the city skyline and the Hudson River. (Anyone who feels bad about Sam getting the crap office alcove for a bedroom at our parents' apartment should know that Czarina's spare bedroom is basically a shrine to Sam—decorated with his music awards, photos of Sam at every recital since he learned to play piano, and the most comfortable bed in the world, picked out by Sam. The duvet on the bed—also chosen by Sam—might as well be embossed with needlepoint hand-stitched by Czarina, announcing: SAM! SAM IS MY FAVORITE!)

Czarina has experienced a good but not lucrative career, so no way has she had the income to support this type of Manhattan real estate. By New York City real estate standards, she's a pauper, but she's lived like a queen, all because when Czarina was a young, broke fashionista, she moved in with her grandparents, into their rent-controlled apartment. And she never left. Hers was the only apartment in the one-hundred-unit building that didn't convert to condo. (Thank Czarina's bulldog lawyer.) Her building is now basically 99 percent rich people, and Czarina. She's the 1 percent at the Stanwyck.

Or, she *was*. After twenty years of buyout offers, Czarina finally agreed to leave her palace. All it took was an extra zero at the end of the financial settlement—before the decimal point. She basically just won the lottery. She's been married five times, and we thought she'd won big when she divorced the Brazilian taxidermist. That settlement was nothing in comparison; she used most of the windfall from that sicko, preserved-moose-head man's money to splurge on a baby grand piano for her Virtuoso Sam, and on a fancy oven for her Chef Sam, so her precious grandson could wow her guests with his amazing meals and music ability. Tonight, I get those all to myself.

I should be mad that Czarina chose my brother over me as her favorite, but even I will acknowledge that Sam is a better person than me. He's everything I'm not. Patient, kind, sweet, talented. *I* would choose him if I was Czarina, too. To be honest, it's a relief that Sam's the star in the family. Being the fuckup bitch is the role I know. I fit into it like anyone's favorite pair of jeans.

I notice the furrow between Sam's eyebrows and the tightening of his forehead. Pre-party jitters. "Where's the spiralizer?"

"What's that?"

"A utensil to spiralize veggies. I thought I might thread in some zucchini to the—"

"Don't. Your menu is perfect as is."

"You used the good silver to set the table, right?"

"Yes. The table looks beautiful. I even fancy-folded the napkins."

"The—"

"Yes, the good ones that Czarina brought back from Dublin. I promise you don't need to halt your cooking to do a last-minute inspection of the dining room. The table is set, the decorations are up, and the cardboard Liberace table center-piece looks better than a flower arrangement."

"Candles!"

"Done."

"Set out the dessert plates and silverware on the buffet."

"Done." I need to stop him from a deeper descent into anxiety about the state of the dining room. "Give me a hint about someone you've invited." Sam's bedroom—er, the guest room—is spread out with my sequined halter tops, feather boas, plaid-patterned polyester bell-bottom pants, and flapper dresses. How can I know the best costume for our party if I don't know who the guests are?

"No. You know the rules. You choose three people, I choose three people. The mix is a surprise—to us, and to them."

"You're going to dress like Ray Charles again, aren't you?" I love my brother's classic suit and tie, of course—but he al-ways wears the same thing. I want to see my brother wearing a sequined cape or a star-spangled-banner leisure suit with beads hanging off the arms. I want him to shake things up for once.

"Yes," says Sam. "But I'll be enjoying the gift of sight. May he rest in peace, Brother Ray." He pauses, and then says, "Please promise me you didn't invite KK."

"I promise," I say.

I totally invited KK!

My guest list:

Kirby Kingsley: Heiress, party girl, my non-sibling BFF. No one likes her besides me. But it's not a party without Kirby. She lives in the Stanwycks' penthouse apartment, with panoramic views of Central Park to the East River, and midtown and uptown to the Hudson River, and probably God, too, if you point their telescope straight up through the glass dome in the ceiling of the atelier room.

Li Zhang: My chem-lab partner. Great at board games. Great conversationalist. Never shows up to a party without a gift of beautiful boxes of sweets from Taiwan for the hostess. Should be invited to *every* party.

Frederyk Podhalanski, aka Freddie: The wild card. He's an exchange student from Poland, living with a family on the Upper East Side. I met him when I was with KK, watching hot guys play basketball in Central Park. Tall, blond, muscled, deep blue eyes, uncomplicated. I'm pretty sure Freddie's the guy I've been looking for—the one who will break my brother's heart.

My brother still hasn't recovered from not getting into Juilliard. He goes to Fiorello LaGuardia High School of Music & Art and Performing Arts, only a few blocks away from Czarina's Palais de Rent Control. Sam should have been *thrilled* not to get into Juilliard. Too fucking close for comfort! He *did* get into Berklee College of Music, in Boston. A whole new city, new adventure, and a prestigious music school, too! But no. My brother opted to go to Hunter College next year, to stay close to home, to play it safe.

Even though I think he should have opted for Berklee, Sam really, truly wants Juilliard, so I want it for him, too. Next year, he'll reapply. Sam should have gotten in. The solution: Sam needs to drop out of his safety zone and go wild for the wrong guy. He needs a recess from the humdrum stream of predictable boys he dates. My brother's heart needs the distraction of infatuation with someone out of his league. To be clear, Freddie's not in a better league than Sam (no one's in a better league than my brother). It's just a different one. I'll call it the League of Ridiculously Beautiful Guys Who Aren't That Bright and Who Will Give My Brother Exactly the Fun Distraction He Needs Before Dumping My Brother When They Realize My Brother Is Too Smart and Good for Them. My brother needs a pointless, pleasurable fling with someone gorgeous and easy.

When Freddie inevitably dumps Sam, the pain will be sharp, but quick. Pain is what makes all the greats great. Known fact. So if pain is what it takes to bring Sam to that pantheon, then I have just the dinner party to give him that necessary shock to the system. It will be a welcome pain compared to the kind Sam inflicts on himself from overthinking and overstressing. And Sam will have loads of fun along the way. You're welcome, brother.

Like Sam, I also experienced the pain of not getting into

my first-choice school, or any of my top-tier choices! I applied to the Sorbonne, the University of Tokyo, and that fancy one in Scotland where Prince William met Princess Kate. But I had no real shot at them. No matter; I don't speak French or Japanese, and let's be real, who even understands Scottish people when they speak? I also didn't get into my second-tier schools—NYU, Skidmore, Fordham. And that's *awesome*. Because now I can hoard all that money I saved babysitting the many little critters who live in the Stanwyck, and not waste it at Quinnipiac University, which is somewhere in Connecticut, I'm told. (I visited but have since tried to forget the experience, because I was basically forced by my parents to go.) It's the only school I got into, and my parents were so relieved, they enrolled me for the fall. I can't even pronounce the school's name. Please.

"Are you sure Czarina hasn't taken a lover?" Sam says. I've got to set him free from attachment to her apron strings, too. When she finds out I broke the leaf on her dining room table when I was setting it, she'll lose it at him. At me, too, of course. But I'm used to it. Sam the Saint is not. It will be healthy. For both of them. Maybe in my future travels I will check out old Freud or Jung's universities in Austria or wherever, because I obviously have huge potential as a psychoanalytic genius.

"Of course I'm not sure!" I say. "She could be bonking every Frenchman with a croissant for all I know!"

"Because every Frenchman has a croissant, right?"

"*Oui!* Don't you know that's what the French Revolution was all about? Life, liberty, *le* perfect flaky croissant."

"Tongs," says Sam.

"Frenchman torture method?"

"No. Hand me the tongs so I can pull out the strips of lasagna from the boiling water."

I hand him the tongs. "That's a whisk, Ilsa." He reaches over me to grab the contraption known as *tongs*. "And I'm telling you, Czarina has taken a lover in Paris."

"You just want to say 'taken a lover.'"

"Guilty. You know me too well."

Maybe Czarina has taken a lover in Paris, but that's not the reason for her trip. She thinks we don't know, but *I* know. Czarina likes to be secretive, but she has no idea what a browser history is, and that she should clear it regularly. Our grandmother is in Paris because she bought a small apartment and plans to retire there, in a little studio with no bedrooms for me or Sam. (Unfortunately, this knowledge came at the cost of also learning that Czarina *really* likes browsing photos of Sean Connery as James Bond wearing barely-there swimmer briefs. And she *loves* porny fan fiction devoted to that most hirsute of the Bond men.) (I'm going to throw up just thinking about what I've seen in her browser history.)

Sam will survive the Paris news. What better place to visit a grandmother? What's really going to finally push Sam out of his comfort zone is when he finds out I am moving into his bedroom at Czarina's, with the new owners, who have invited me to be their family's nanny after Czarina moves out. Sam has too much talent and potential to be stuck in the same old place; I'm fine there.

Tonight is our chance to celebrate our last twin dinner party here. Lasagna, booze, chocolates, with our friends and some strangers. Tonight we can swing from the chandeliers like we're Liberace.

Tomorrow we can deal with the heartbreak and the humdrum.

two

SAM

Dinner parties always seem like a good idea until you have an hour until the guests arrive and you realize you have about four hours' worth of things left to do. Life becomes a whirl of counter-space choreography, stovetop stress, and table-setting trauma. I want everything to be perfect, and I also know this is an impossible and even cruel thing to want. Still, there's something deep inside me that won't let go. If things are imperfect, it won't—can't—be my fault.

Ilsa, bless her, is trying to aid me. Unfortunately, her aid is coming in the form of sartorial suggestion.

"Why aren't you wearing your black velvet? They'll be here any moment. You're still in jeans."

I am not wearing my black velvet because the lemon tart requires a dusting of confectioners' sugar in about two minutes. It will take about two minutes to explain this to Ilsa, so I try to shoo her from the kitchen instead, telling her that she should make sure the dinner party playlist is to her liking. My mood is all Glass, and if she wants to add swing to the thing, it's better for her to do it now than to make a scratch mid-song.

My stress gets more level when I am alone in the kitchen. I like being alone in the kitchen. My thoughts fit well into the sound of bubbling, boiling, and refrigeration. I can be the conductor of this minor orchestra.

It's only when other people get involved that the conducting becomes unwieldy, and arrangements get messy.

I don't know who Ilsa's invited, although I suspect that, despite her denial, KK will soon besmirk our doorway with her usual gusts of privilege. Ilsa can't resist KK—she's the fashion plate my sister eats off of, her droll model. I personally can't fathom how a girl so rich can also be so rich with complaint. But she's never wanted me or anyone else to like her. I guess there's some power that comes from that. Only I'm not really sure what you can use that power for.

My guest list is, I hope, a little more amenable to amiability.

First, there's my best friend, Parker, since even though Ilsa placed him on the Banished Guest List, I am not having this last dinner party without him. Ilsa claims he broke her heart, but she needs to get over it. Mostly because the breakup was totally her fault, and nearly ended my friendship with him, which wasn't fair.

Next up is Jason. I figured if I was inviting one of Ilsa's

exes, I should balance it out with one of mine. Although it's not really the same, since Jason and I managed to stay friends. He'd had this whole I'm-going-to-Tufts-and-you're-going-to-Berklee! plan, and when I decided to stay in Manhattan, it was like I'd slapped his future, which in turn said *oh-no-you-didn't* and stormed out the door. This left the present standing in the middle of the room, slight and awkward. Jason withdrew his application for soul mate, and we went from there. Still looking for true love, but not with each other.

Which *maybe* leads me to my wild card: Subway Boy. I've been seeing him on the 1 train for the past few months. And around the city, especially around Lincoln Center. Sometimes he's carrying a violin case. I have mapped more fantasies out onto Subway Boy than I care to admit. And after a while, I saw that he was recognizing me as much as I was recognizing him.

Still, I didn't want to ruin it by talking to him. Until, last week, he was right there when I got on board the train, and it was like the party invitation in my pocket began to vibrate. Before I could tell myself to halt, halt, *halt,* I was handing it to him and telling him he should come.

"There's no RSVP," he said when he finished reading it.

He didn't look at me like I was bad crazy. He looked at me like I was good crazy. Bold crazy. Romantic crazy.

"Regrets only," I told him.

"Well," he said with a smile, "I can't say I have any regrets."

As we hit his stop, I ventured a "See you later?"

"Absolutely," he replied.

And that, it seemed, was that. I haven't seen him since. I'm not even sure he'll show up. I'm afraid that, if he does, Ilsa will ask me his name.

I have no idea what his name is.

Nor, for that matter, do I know if he's vegan. Or only eats meat. Or is lactose intolerant. Gluten agnostic. Kale monogamous. So I'm making a little of everything, which adds up to way too much.

"You do realize we're only having six guests?" Ilsa, back in the kitchen, asks as I bedevil an egg. The flapper dress she has on would make even Clara Bow fall silent in respect. "And none of them, at least on my list, eats this much."

I can never keep my sister out of the kitchen for that long, not when we're the only two people home. It's not that she likes watching me cook. And it's certainly not that she likes assisting. She just hates being in a room by herself.

"I've invited Rudolph Tate," I say. "He requires at least six servings."

This is mean. Rudolph Tate eats like a bird and looks like a bird and flew the coop after two chirpy dates with me. Ilsa had set us up, and since it was only the latest in a mess of maladroit matches, I asked her to never, ever set me up again. It was getting to be that when a male at Ilsa's school came out of the closet, the first thing he found was my sister standing by the closet door, saying she had someone he should really, really meet.

"If you'd invited Rudy, I would have heard about it," Ilsa

15

says, her faith in gossip unwavering. "He's the apple of #Stantastic's rebounding eye now. And #Stantastic tweets anything that makes him jealous."

My date with #Stantastic had been even worse than my date with Rudolph. As we were talking over dinner, he kept typing it all down on his phone. I tried not to give him any material, and as a result ended up being called #sleepyandhollow when he gave everyone his side of the story. Amazingly, he didn't understand why I passed on a second date. I know this because he told his (fifty-six) followers he was #Stantagonized by the fact that I hadn't been #Stantalized.

I study Ilsa's face, to see if she's invited Rudolph or #Stantastic. It's looking like a no. I'm relieved . . . and still a little worried about who else that leaves.

I check the oven, and at least everything there seems to be going according to plan. Satisfied by the tick of the timer, I sugar the tart and give the Waldorf salad an extra toss, making sure the lemon-juiced apples haven't defied me and started to brown. I know it's time for me to take off my apron and get into host mode . . . but I want to linger in the kitchen a little bit longer. It's so much safer here.

"This is it," I tell Ilsa. "Our last dinner party of high school."

This is the beginning of all the goodbyes. I've been preparing for them, in my own way. I'm ready for graduation. But I'm not ready for life to change so much, so soon.

I can't say any of this to Ilsa because it's too depressing.

And my sister does not like to be depressed. I may be the gay one, but she's the one who lives by gaiety. Carefree and careless, the life of the party trying to make a party out of her life—that's my unidentical twin, with her unidentity.

"It all looks so *grand*," she says, trying on the last word like a little girl tries on her mother's shoes.

Or her grandmother's shoes. I guess we're both wearing our grandmother's shoes. Look at me, with all of my culinary creations—I want to dazzle. Look at Ilsa, in her shimmering flapper dress—she wants to be dazzling.

"The humdrum won't know what hit it," I promise her.

"It won't dare set foot in this apartment, not while we're around."

"It shall be a night to remember."

She nods. "For the ages."

I make one last check that everything is boiling, brewing, and baking as it should. With ten minutes left, I retreat to my room to change. My clothes hang ready on the closet door. Black suit. White shirt. Dark blue tie. I always wear this outfit because I don't think I look as good in anything else. And I want to look good tonight.

Despite myself, I have hopes.

I'm far from certain that he's going to show up. This boy whose name I don't even know.

I told Parker about it, of course. I'm sure one of the reasons I did was because I knew it would make him think I had the potential to be at least momentarily brave. After months of him telling me to talk to Subway Boy, of him threatening to

17

go up to Subway Boy and say, "Hey, my friend here likes you," I finally made the move.

And now, the waiting.

You're good, Parker tells me. I need to borrow his voice sometimes, when I don't trust my own.

Eight minutes. I button my buttons.

Six minutes. I tie my tie.

Five minutes. I—

I—

I can't go out there. I can't do this. I can't. I really can't. I'm going to tell Ilsa I'm feeling sick. I can't let any of this happen. Whatever's going to happen, I don't want it to happen. This was such a mistake. I am such a fraud. I want to stay in the kitchen. I don't want anyone else to come in. I don't want to have to talk to anybody. My body knows this. My body is shutting down, saying, *That's enough for you, Sam.* I tried to believe I could. I tried to trick myself. But the only thing I'm smart at is knowing when I'm going to fail. There's no way to disguise that. I am going to fail.

Four minutes.

I can't fool anybody.

Three minutes.

Ilsa is calling my name. I am trying to do all the things the doctor told me to do. Slow down. Deep breaths. Affirm. I can do this. Whether or not he comes. Whether or not this is the end of our dinner parties. Whether or not Ilsa appreciates it.

Two minutes. I consult my mirror.

18

I do look better than I usually do.

I remember that at some point in the night, I'll be taking the jacket off. So I'm careful. Very careful.

I make sure my sleeves are rolled down and buttoned, covering any lingering trace of my damage.

One minute. The buzzer buzzes.

The first guest has arrived.

three

ILSA

I open the door and immediately I know.

This must be Wild Card Boy.

I know because he has the shy, sweet look of so many of Sam's city crushes. Starbucks Boy. AMC Theatre Boy. Pret a Manger Boy. Terminal 5 Boy. Trader Joe's Boy.

Whoever this guy standing here is, he's exactly why I've invited Freddie. Our dinner party absolutely needs a Smoking Hot, Seemed Uncomplicated on the B-ball Court but Could Be Deeply Disturbed Eastern European Guy to break Sam's infatuation mold of Nice, Safe Boys.

Wild Card Boy is long and skinny, just like the others, and he's wearing black jeans (not garish at all—did he even read the invitation?), just like the others. Wild Card's major improvement is his white T-shirt picturing a hipster black cat standing on its hind legs, playing a fiddle with its front legs. The shirt says I PAWS FOR BLUEGRASS. Wild Card Boy is pale-skinned like he's a shut-in, with shaggy ginger hair and a scruffy ginger beard and deep green eyes. With his red-orange hair and black skinny jeans, Wild Card Boy looks like an upside-down pumpkin. But Wild Card Boy is highly cute, and has a big, warm smile that I try not to find suspicious. He holds a violin case.

"Hi," I say. "Welcome. I'm Ilsa. And you are . . . ?"

"Johan!" he says jovially. "Delighted to be here, but disappointed that Czarina won't be here! With a name like that—"

I interrupt. "You have a funny accent. Are you Australian?"

"South African."

"Isn't that like the same?"

"In no way whatsoever."

"You're a long way from home, Johan. What brought you to New York?"

"Juilliard. I play the violin."

"Classical?"

"At school, yes. But American bluegrass is where my heart is."

I hear Sam's voice. "Stop with the interrogation, Ilsa! Let the poor guy in already. He's not a vampire." He stands behind me and loudly whispers in my ear, "Is he?"

I turn around and see Sam wearing his favorite suit, with his regrettably red-cheeked blush revealing his every feeling. *Hope! Anticipation!* The kid's never going to be a poker champion.

21

"I think this one's mortal," I tell Sam. But just to be sure, I ask Johan, "You're not a vampire, are you?"

"No," says Johan, "despite how tempting your neck is looking." He winks at me, then at Sam. "His neck, too."

What. A. Pro. My favorite guest of the night, already.

"Come in, please," I say, holding the door open for him to step through.

Johan carries in his violin case but nothing else so far as I can see. You can tell a lot about a person by the type of gift they bring for their host (Pret a Manger Boy—leftover cookies; Terminal 5 Boy—flowers; Starbucks Boy—gingerbread syrup), or if they don't (Trader Joe's Boy—the worst). I suppose Johan is in the Don't category. Maybe they don't bring gifts in South Africa. Not like I throw a party just to get the gifts. (But please bring those amazing chocolates, Li Zhang.)

"This is your granny's actual apartment?" Johan asks as we lead him through the foyer and into the living room, which is at the building's corner and offers views of the Empire State Building and midtown Manhattan to the south and the Hudson River to the west. "Everyone I know lives in dirty dorms or crowded shares in Bushwick."

"The apartment's been in the family for three generations. Before everything got so crazy expensive around here," says Sam, sounding like he's apologizing for Czarina not living up to starving-artist, bohemian standards.

"Rent controlled," I add, so Johan will know we're only surrounded by lucky moneybags folk. We're not them.

Sam hates hates hates when I bring up the rent-control

22

subject—especially so soon—to total strangers, but I've found it's a good way to appraise their character right away. Either they're happy for you or they literally hate your guts for having such luck in your family. It's better to know right away. What's it matter, anyway? The luck's all ending.

Johan says, "*This* is what rent controlled means? I've heard about it, but I thought it had to be an urban myth."

"It's a rarity, but not a myth. And it's all going bye-bye," I say, pointing to the movers' boxes against the far corner of the living room wall. "This whole apartment cost our grand-mother significantly less every month than you probably pay for a tiny dorm room you share with a snoring roommate, or mice, or both."

"I have both!" Johan says.

"May I get you a drink?" Sam asks Johan, trying to change the subject. "We have sparkling water, pomegranate juice, ginger ale. . . ."

"Beer?" Johan asks. With his accent, the word sounds like *beeyrah?*

"Sorry," says Sam the Saint. "I promised our grandmother we wouldn't serve alcohol."

"I'll get you one," I say. "Sam Adams or Sierra Nevada?" Sam and I have a tacit understanding: He repeats the party line about Czarina's rules, then looks the other way when I disobey them.

"You choose," says Johan. "Thanks, mate."

I leave for the kitchen, to give Sam some time alone with Johan. New guests—especially if they're not from the city—always want a tour of the grand, chipping-away old apartment. I hope Johan appreciates my party-decorating efforts. I pinned decorations across the living room walls, picturing Liberace in his many years of spectacularly garish fashions. I dangled small, mirrored disco balls from the chandelier over the dining room table. I stocked the bathrooms with Czarina's best hand towels from Ireland, and stocked the bathroom vanity drawers with Advil (for guests who can't handle the booze), Pepto-Bismol (can't handle Sam's cooking), and a colorful array of condoms (want to get handled).

The house phone in the kitchen that connects our apartment to the building lobby rings, like it's still 1956 and people don't have cell phones.

"Hello?" I answer.

"Announcing . . . ," the doorman starts to say.

"Please don't announce, Bert. Please just send them up. Thank you!"

I hang up the phone and pull out a Sam Adams from the fridge for me and one for Johan, taking a count of the beers in there so I know how many I'll have to replace with swiped stock from KK's parents before Czarina gets home. They never notice the beer missing any more than they notice that KK practically subsists exclusively on sushi and frozen Jell-O pops.

As I head to the front door, I hear Sam playing the piano in the study, Duke Ellington's "Prelude to a Kiss." Bold move, brother, so early in the night! Such a sweet, hopeful melody. I'm encouraged. This is going to be our best dinner party ever. I can feel it.

I wait for the doorbell to ring, as I always do, resisting the urge to open the front door and look down the hallway to see our guests disembarking from the elevator onto the eighth floor. A good hostess welcomes her guests but doesn't seem desperate for them. I look at myself in the mirror in the foyer, blotting my matte burgundy lips, de-smudging the black kohl lined beneath my eyes, and smoothing down the black bangs of my newly cut, razor-sharp twenties showgirl bob, whose ends come to points on either side of my chin.

I wish upon the next guest: *Please be Wilson Salazar, please be Wilson Salazar.* Johan, one of Sam's three mystery guests, has been accounted for, and I can already tell Johan is awesome. Sam will obviously invite Jason Goldstein-Chung, because Jason is Sam's habitual safe choice. Jason is like the comfort food of ex-boyfriends. That leaves one more guest on Sam's list, and I salivate with hope that Sam finally extended an invitation to Wilson Salazar, the most talented and hottest actor in the senior class at LaGuardia. Wilson killed as Macbeth last fall. He broke my heart in *West Side Story* this spring.

The doorbell rings. I cross my fingers and softly sing a little prayer invoking Wilson Salazar's presence. *"Tonight, tonight / It all began tonight."*

I open the door.

DAMMIT!

"You're looking very fetching, Ilsa," Parker Jordan manages to say, seemingly effortlessly, while holding a rose stem between his teeth. He's wearing the sequined, Michael Jackson–style black-and-white tuxedo he always wore when we used to compete as ballroom dance partners. He's let his hair grow to high-top, *Fresh Prince of Bel-Air* height, the style Parker always used to tease me that he'd finally get when I wasn't telling the barber how to shave his head anymore. Wish = fulfilled.

I grab the red rose from his mouth and throw it down the hallway. "Fetch this, Parker!" I say.

Parker laughs. "Oh, Ilsa. Bygones already."

"You're early," I tell Parker.

"What time was I supposed to arrive?"

"Never."

"Right on time!" Parker says.

He doesn't wait for me to usher him, but boldly steps past me, walks through the foyer and into the living room with the ease of someone who's been here a million times. I close the front door and follow him. He hands me a brown paper shopping bag. "Here. These are from Mom and Dad." His ears take notice of the sound of the piano-playing coming from the study. "Ellington. Nice start, Sam."

I snatch the bag from Parker's hand and don't bother with "Thanks." I'll save that for an email, later, directly to his parents. The bag has two stacked boxes inside it, and I know exactly what's in them: a sweet potato pie and a lemon chess pie, my favorites from Parker's parents' vegan soul food café in Hell's Kitchen.

I guess if they've sent my favorite pies, they've forgiven me for the video I posted of Parker breaking up with me, which went viral (at least among everyone we know, and a good deal of Manhattan). According to Sam's report, that video has caused Parker to be besieged by hordes of angry girls recognizing him on the street and repeating his line back to him: "It's not you, it's me. . . ." Then the girls swat at him and shrill, "JERK!" (I'm pleased every time I get this report. Sisters who've been dumped, unite!)

I guess if Parker's here tonight, he's forgiven me, too.

I don't know how long it will take me to forgive Sam, though. He knows I have a moratorium on seeing Parker again until the school year is officially over. I don't want to be so blatantly reminded of Parker until after prom night, until after senior week, until after graduation and all the things Parker and I were supposed to share together.

"No gifts to me from your parents?" Parker teases. I resist a laugh. No one was more relieved when we broke up than my parents. Relieved for Parker, not me.

"They're at Home Depot right now looking for just the right ax to bash your high-top down to baldy height."

"Tell them no interest on purchases over $250 if they use their HD credit card. They oughta splurge on that plasma welder your dad's always dreamed of owning to finally shut your damn mouth."

My parents don't even know where Home Depot is.

Sam and Johan return from the study and Sam introduces Johan to Parker.

"You look familiar," Johan tells Parker. "Do I know you from somewhere? Like a commercial?"

I try to telepathically message Johan the punch line of his recognition. *It's not you, it's me. . . . JERK!* But Johan doesn't receive it, and Sam quickly changes the subject. "Ilsa. Where have we decided to check the phones tonight?"

After four dinner parties ago, when #Stantastic #live tweeted #Stanstunnedbyboredom all night, we banned cell phones from our parties, which improved our parties to an infinite degree. Now our guests savor their food instead of just Instagramming it. They enjoy the city view instead of getting lost on their phones trying to add "@theStanwyck" location to their Facebook posts. They *talk* to each other.

Now I have a change of heart. "Let's not put away the phones tonight." I maybe can't handle a whole evening of witty conversation with guests when suddenly I'd rather spend the night crying in my room because Parker is here, and he's probably going to talk all night about what amazing (not reckless) girl he's taking to prom, or about all the first- and second-tier colleges he got into because what Ivy League school wouldn't want a half-Dominican, half–African American male valedictorian who's also a star lacrosse player, a champion ballroom dancer (in his previous, Ilsa life), and the son of vegan baking royalty.

I'm going to be a hostess like Czarina tonight. I'm going to act like everything's just grand even though I can't believe Sam invited Parker. I feel so betrayed. Much as I think it would be healthy for Sam to have his heart broken, I would never then *invite* the cause of his pain to his own party after the breakup! This hurts.

"Please, let's put away the phones!" says Johan. "I've always been curious to go to a party without them. I know, we could lock the phones in my violin case." He walks over to where his violin case rests on the floor by the foyer. As he's about to open the case, Johan looks up at us and says, "I didn't know what to bring as a host gift. So I brought the 'garish' inside here."

four

SAM

Once upon a time, there was a marketing genius. And this marketing genius noticed that boys wouldn't play with dolls, so dolls for boys needed a new name. He decided to call them *action figures,* and because of this, boys began to play with dolls. The marketing genius must have been proud.

I wonder what this marketing genius would think of what's inside Johan's violin case. Because these are definitely action figures. Same height. Same plastic.

Only, all of these action figures are Dolly Parton.

It's not just the chests, which would make a shrimp out of Barbie's. It's the whole package. Petite and big and bold all at the same time.

There's Dolly in her coat of many colors, a poor, sweet girl about to make millions.

There's Dolly singing "I Will Always Love You"—which you know because an angel-winged Whitney is smiling behind her.

There's Dolly standing on a desk in a triumphant 9 to 5 pose. Her boss cowers, hog-tied below.

And finally, there's Dolly arm-wrestling . . . someone.

"That's Sylvester Stallone," Johan explains in his charming woodwind voice. "From *Rhinestone*."

Rhinestone.

I am nearly at a loss for words. "You've built Dollywood. In a violin case."

"I like to think of it as a fiddle case. But yes. When you specified garish, I assumed you meant *awesome*."

Parker gives me one of his *oh, so this is what white people do in their free time* looks, but I can tell he's glad Subway Boy hasn't proven to be the instant disappointment that most Subway Boys must be once you have them over for dinner. Ilsa looks annoyed—maybe because Parker's within ejection range without a trapdoor in sight, or maybe because a stranger has just upped the garish ante, and she's not sure how many chips she has left to place.

"Let me get you that beer," she says, off to the kitchen before Johan can tell her the hair in the Dollys' wigs was spun from unicorn tears.

"I'm going to go see if she needs help carrying that beer," Parker says, following.

Johan moves to close the violin case, and I cry out, way too loud, "No! Don't!" Then, as if to compound this manic burst of uncoolness, I walk over to the piano and clear a place for the case . . . by sweeping off all the sheet music with my arm, as if I'm in some retirement home's production of *Amadeus*. As a result, the Goldberg Variations scatter through the air, Debussy ducks for cover under the bench, and Muhly mulishly meanders toward Czarina's beloved lime green couch.

If Johan is alarmed, he doesn't show it. He gives the Dolly clones their pride of place. He casually plays a few notes on the piano in honor of the installation. I hear the words in my head.

Islands in the stream.

That is what we are.

If Ilsa were here, she'd be on the piano, singing along.

I—

I—

I look away. I know a new person is supposed to mean a new start. But I'm still me, and eventually he will see that.

"Do you want something to drink?" I ask.

He looks at me like I've made a joke. Then he realizes maybe I haven't.

Right. Pretty much the only fact I know about him is that he wants a beer.

"It'll be any minute now," I say, looking down. I am rolling over Beethoven. I want to apologize to him.

"I loved hearing you play," Johan says.

"I loved the feeling of you standing right behind me as I played," I don't reply. "There was even a moment when I forgot to worry about impressing you and actually enjoyed myself."

It had been so simple. He'd seen the piano. Asked me who played.

All I had to do was say, "I do."

All I had to do was sit there and let the song happen.

No. *Make* the song happen.

"I gave it up," I find myself saying to him now.

There are so many things I am saying underneath this. Mostly to myself. But beneath that. Something I am trying to give him. Some indication of who I am, of what this is.

"When?" he asks.

"A couple of years ago," I tell him. Even though it was actually only seven months ago, after I sabotaged myself out of music school and vowed never to perform in public—never to be put on display like that, with all of the pressure—ever again.

"But clearly you didn't give it up entirely?" He lifts some fallen notes from the floor.

"That was the weird thing. I gave up on it, but it didn't give up on me."

"Music is inescapable, isn't it?"

The way he says it, I can tell there are things he already knows.

I nod. Even if I wasn't playing in public anymore, it was still a part of my most private self.

He's looking at me with such curiosity. I was Subway Boy to him, too, and now I am not. I have yet to be determined.

We have yet to be determined.

The doorbell marks the arrival of another guest. I pause, trying to sense some movement from the kitchen. When I don't notice any, I make an excuse to Johan and head for the door.

I am sorry to leave him. Which seems prematurely foolish, but there it is.

When I get to the door, I open it and find Ilsa's friend Li, who is usually a model of sense and sensibility.

But tonight she's dressed in what can only be called a slutty French maid outfit. By which I mean: one of those Halloween costumes that's supposed to look like a French maid, only sluttier.

She takes one look at my outfit and another at my face. Then she says, "It isn't a costume party, is it?"

I shake my head.

"Why did I think it was a costume party?" she asks.

I have no answer for this.

"I live in Jackson Heights."

Meaning: There is no turning around and going back home. This is what she's wearing tonight.

"And I'll never fit into your sister's clothes."

Meaning: No, really, this is what she's wearing tonight.

"Well, it *is* garish," I say. "I'm sure there were at least three guys at each of Liberace's parties wearing the exact same thing."

I can see her compartmentalize her embarrassment. I envy that.

She holds up a bag. "I brought the chocolate your sister loves."

I gesture behind me. "She's in the kitchen. Just make sure she shares."

34

Li reaches behind her and pulls out a second bag.

"This is for the rest of us."

Such a good guest.

She is wearing heels that I sense are a little higher than her usual elevation. So there's a certain teeter as she angles toward the kitchen, bags in hand. I close the apartment door behind her.

"Parker's here, too," I tell her. As if to confirm this, there is a crash of breaking glass in the kitchen, and my sister shouting something that sounds demonstrably like *ASSHOLE*.

"Maybe I'll hold off," Li says. "This chocolate is too good to be thrown at someone's face."

"This way," I tell her.

When I get back into the piano room, the sheet music is all stacked in a neat column alongside Johan's violin case, like an office tower built over the Guggenheim.

"Johan, Li. Li, Johan," I say.

As Li is shaking his hand, she asks, "And how do you two know each other?"

"Mass transit," Johan replies, offering no further explanation.

The noise from the kitchen has reached the decibel level known by musicologists as *hollering*. The doorbell takes this as its cue to ring again.

I assume Ilsa will use this as her excuse to leave the kitchen. She does not.

"I'll get it," I say. As if either Li or Johan could be viable candidates for the task.

I figure it's going to be Jason, but when I open the door, I find someone who is not even remotely Jason. On the hotness scale, Jason may have been a firecracker . . . but this guy's the sun. He is wearing clothes, but my body reacts like he isn't. My gaze rises from his strong shoulders to focus on his face.

"Hello," I say. And it sounds like *hell*, because the *oh* comes out so low.

I see he has one of our invitations in his hand. This has to be one of Ilsa's guests.

Then his other hand gets my attention.

Because—

It has a sock on it.

A white tube sock with green button eyes.

And a red-stitched mouth.

And brown yarn hair.

"I hope we're in the right place," the sock says.

It has a disturbingly attractive voice. English as a second language . . . with Sexy Beast being the first.

"Excuse me?" I say. Because nine out of ten times, when you're confronted with a sock puppet, that is the only valid response.

"This is Ilsa's party, isn't it?" the sock continues. I look up at the godlike guy, and his lips aren't moving.

"It *is* Ilsa's party," I say. I am *not* talking to the hand. I am talking to the hot guy who is looking at me like his hand isn't talking to me. "I'm her brother, Sam."

"Nice to meet you," the sock says. It holds out its hand. Which is his pinkie. Under a sock.

I look at the guy, as if to say, *You can't be serious.*

36

He looks back at me, as if to say, *This is my life choice and you must respect it.*

I shake the sock's hand-pinkie.

"I'm Caspian," it says. "This is Frederyk. He met Ilsa when he was playing basketball. I am not allowed to accompany him on the court, so I missed the chance to meet her. But I am happy to meet you now."

"Come in," I say. "*Please.*"

I am fairly certain that Ilsa's wild card is a bit more wild than she imagined.

Or she's fucking with me.

Which isn't nice.

She knows how I get.

She knows.

"What a lovely home," Caspian tells me, looking around with his button eyes.

"Thank you," I say.

Can she be fucking with me?

No. Yes.

If this is an act, he's *really* good at it.

"I must admit that I knew you were Ilsa's brother. I have heard such lovely things about you."

No. No no no. That's too much.

"Did she put you up to this?" I ask Frederyk. "She did, didn't she? This is going to end up on the Internet, isn't it? Where's the camera?"

Frederyk smiles sweetly at me.

No. This is my life choice and you must respect it.

"You're even cuter than she said you were," Caspian tells me. Wild. Card.

I don't know whether to take them—*him*—straight to the kitchen or back to the piano room.

"What the hell?" a voice intones.

Six eyes—two of them buttons—turn to the still-open front door.

"I've only been here six seconds, and already I'm bored," KK bitches.

Hard as it is to believe, she's wearing a French maid outfit, too.

five

ILSA

"ASSHOLE!" I shriek at Parker after he makes the most provocative and completely absurd request I've ever heard from him. I take an icy beer glass from the freezer and lob it directly toward his high-top 'fro head. He quickly ducks. The glass hits the kitchen tile behind Parker's head and shatters, as it always does. It's been so long since Parker and I have had this kind of fight, all the old broken beer glasses have been replaced, and I don't remember where to buy these particular ones anymore. Hopefully Czarina won't notice we're down to three German beer glasses in the freezer. Hopefully this level of fight no longer heats me so hard I want to jump Parker's bones immediately after breaking something.

"Chill. The. Fuck. Out," Parker tells me, but he's completely unfazed, which agitates me even more. He walks to the pantry, pulls out the broom and pan, and begins sweeping the broken glass into the broom pan, way too comfortable with this old habit. "Do you want to do it or not?"

"NOT!" I declare, because my pride is speaking for me.

But my heart longs to do it. My body literally aches for it.

"Come on, Ils," he says, laying on his sweetest voice, which he knows I can never resist. If I was wearing a button-down blouse, the button at my boobs would pop open right now, just from hearing Parker use this particular cajoling tone, which worked so effectively on me in the past. "Once more, for old times' sake."

"I don't remember how," I lie. It's so long since I've done it. Like, since Parker and I broke up.

There have been other boys since. I even did it with KK once. But none could do it with me like Parker could. And the KK time involved a lot of Jäger shots to get me into position.

Parker dumps the broken glass into the trash, then steps behind me and lightly gyrates his pelvis against my rear. "Of course you remember," he whispers in my ear. The feel of his breath scorches my neck, and the rest of my body tingles. He places his arms around my waist, so boldly, and I don't resist. For a moment, I clasp my hands over his to tie him around me. The old rhythm of desire and familiarity returns too easily. I want to believe this is right. I want to believe so badly that this could happen.

But I don't trust. I remember how much I thought he loved me. I remember how much I knew I loved him.

I pull away from him and turn around. "Why now?"

"I think it'd be fun," he says, turning the pleading tone up to its highest decibel of smooth sexiness.

"Don't you have some other girl to do it with?"

"None who move like you. You know that."

I do know that.

Light bulb! *Ding ding ding!* I can't believe I'm even considering this, but I say, "It would have to involve the cats. It—"

"No," he interrupts. "No cats. They ruin it for me every time."

Got him.

"Cats," I say. "Or no Ilsa."

He exhales deeply. "Okay. Cats."

"I'll think about it."

But I'm already imagining the new moves I'm going to amaze Parker with. Since we broke up, I've taken up barre classes, and snoozer yoga (mostly for the nap time at the end, which feels like the only time I ever rest), and even dabbled in some pole dancing classes. I now have bendy moves in my repertoire that Parker's never dared dream his partner could do, because his subconscious doesn't yet know they're even possible.

"Don't think about it. Go change now," Parker suggests, knowing full well I stored my show dresses at Czarina's and that once I make the change, there's nothing to think about anymore. I'm totally in.

I will go change. But not for a few minutes yet. I want Parker to yearn and hope and wait. I want him to remember what that feels like. I won't give him the satisfaction too quickly. Prolonging his wait, making him unsure if he'll achieve the conquest he so ardently desires, was always my favorite dance with him. But oh, what glorious results.

I look down at my sad sack of a little silver, sparkly flapper dress. An hour ago it seemed so cute. But my dinner party invite was a call to arms for garish, and then the hostess herself didn't live up to the invitation's promise. An outfit this boring? It's like I let Sam pick my attire. What was I thinking? I specified the party was a recess from the humdrum, and then I outfitted myself in humdrum. Obviously I needed Parker here to remind me to unlock the cats from the garment bag where they've been hiding in Czarina's closet since Parker and I broke up. Of course! I get it now. GARISH. Let's go, Ilsa! The cats are coming out of retirement. Meow for the wow.

Czarina is a great seamstress, and she created a fabulous A-line cocktail dress for me with fabric I found at a cheap fabric-bolt store in the Garment District. The pattern on the off-white fabric is called AccessorCat, and it features pastel-colored illustrations of various cats wearing various accessories: a gray-and-tan-striped tabby cat wearing bright blue eyeglasses, an orange marble cat wearing a debonair purple scarf, a black cat wearing an emerald green cowboy hat. "If Princess Grace Kelly was a crazy cat lady," is how Czarina characterized the atrociously awesome dress. It was my favorite to wear when Parker and I competed in ballroom dancing competitions, until he forbade it, saying just the sight of it had made him allergic to animals. But if he's bold enough to request that I come out of retirement and be his dance partner once again at some mystery dance-off on the Lower East Side later tonight, surely he's man enough to handle the cat dress again.

So what if my initial reaction to his request was typically Ilsa knee-jerk rage. I'll grow out of it at some point, Czarina promises. (We both secretly fear I won't.) Now I'm seeing the potential. A midnight-hour dance-off downtown, one last spin with my once and never again true love.

YES.

I won't commit just yet. I'll let Parker know that I'm in later, after the appetizer course is served.

Parker reaches to the kitchen counter and picks up the steel shaker that Sam had been using to sprinkle powdered sugar over the lemon tart. He shakes a dash of powdered sugar on my hair. "Change now," Parker requests. "So I know you're in. Pretty please?" He shakes an extra dash of sugar onto my head, and some of it lands on my eyelids and nose. He presses his index finger to my nose, lifts off some sugar, and then offers his finger to my lips, knowing full well how hungry I am.

I lick the sugar from Parker's finger—delicious! (the sugar, and the finger)—a ruse to grab the shaker from his other hand at the same time. I dash sugar on top of his head as Parker wrestles me to grab the shaker back. We are laughing and fighting for supremacy of the shaker when we hear KK announce her arrival in the kitchen.

"Enough with the food fight!" KK bellows. "People are waiting on beers! Be a proper hostess, bitch!" Parker and I separate, giving KK and her French maid's outfit a long stare.

It's not so much garish as full-on slutty. Classic lame-o Halloween, not classic Liberace. KK points at me. "There's a pudgy girl in the living room also wearing the same outfit. Fix it." She walks between Parker and me, giving him a cursory nudge. "You again. Ugh." She reaches the fridge, pulls out a light beer, pops it open, takes a swig, then asks, "Is something burning in here?"

As if he heard her from the other room, Sam comes rushing into the kitchen and opens the oven. "Shit! Some cheese exploded onto the bottom of the oven."

"Is that lasagna?" KK asks him.

"Yes," Sam says as he pulls the tray from the oven.

"Obviously you forgot that I'm gluten- and dairy-free," says KK.

"I didn't," says Sam. He looks toward me. "Help!" he pleads.

He means, *Get everyone out of the kitchen.* Dinner parties have a peculiar habit in which all the guests congregate in the kitchen while Sam is trying to coordinate food preparation, blocking his way and commenting on his concoctions before he's ready for judgment. "We should just call them kitchen parties," he's often lamented.

"Everyone to the living room!" I declare as a faint smell of smoke wafts out from the burnt cheese at the bottom of the oven.

"The sock puppet has arrived," Sam tells me.

"Huh?" I remember no such Wild Card. Sam must mean Jason Goldstein-Chung has arrived. Jason always has some weird trick up his sleeve—or sock, as the case must be.

"Go see," Sam says. He pulls some beers from the fridge—a sure sign that he's starting to stress, if he's taking direct responsibility for alcohol consumption—and hands them to me. "Go forth and entertain your guests, Ilsa. *All* of them."

I start to lead Parker and KK out of the kitchen when I hear a weird sound that's somewhere between a belch and a puke. I look to Parker, then KK, then Sam, but none of them looks squeamish. The sound grows louder, and we all look around, trying to identify the sound, and then it identifies itself.

A small volcano of bilge erupts from the kitchen sink.

I'm no cook, but I'm pretty sure if our sink is backed up, that will make further food preparation difficult, if not impossible.

"Fuck!" Sam exclaims.

KK says, "Hallelujah! Tell your chef dad to come over and bring a proper meal to replace the one you've ruined. Gluten-free, please. We're not savages!"

Sam says, "Sorry, KK. The folks are at the annual Gluten-Glee Carb Fest in Wheatland, North Dakota, this weekend. Sbarro and Papa John's are headlining this year. Cap'n Crunch is the opening act!"

KK throws her hands over her ears. "Stop it! I'm getting fatter just listening to the latest lie about your parents." KK never quite believes our parents exist. They do. They just rarely come to the Stanwyck. Probably because it hurts too much knowing they'll never inherit it. And it would be a compliment to say that KK is their least favorite of my friends.

You'd never find my parents trolling opportunities for more KK time.

Sam pops open a beer and takes a hearty swig. He never drinks at our parties. "Stress," he sighs.

I counter-sigh in support. And triumph.

This is bad.

But could also be excellent.

Finally, my brother may be ready to let loose.

six

SAM

Deep breaths.
  I must.
  Take.
  Deep.
  Breaths.
  It's only water. We don't need water. I just have to pretend
I'm in droughty Los Angeles.
  The food has all been made. There's bottled water in the
fridge and in the cupboards. We don't have to clean up right
away.
  Everything.
  Is.
  Under.
  Control.
  Only.

My mind.

Is.

Not.

Under.

Control.

I take another swig of beer, grimacing as it goes down. I am only drinking it because I don't like it. A punishment of hops. This way I'm not going to want more.

I call down to Bert, in the lobby, for help, but he can't leave the door. He also tells me Jason is on his way up. I wonder if Bert remembers Jason's name from back when Jason and I were dating, when he'd visit all the time. Or maybe it's been long enough that Jason had to remind Bert who he was.

Even though the sink is sunk and my despair has definitely been tapped, I still manage to salvage the lasagna and get the rest of the food in order. I time Jason's steps perfectly, and open the door just as he's about to ring the bell.

He jumps a little. "You scared me," he says.

I hear it as *You scarred me* and don't know what to say.

He looks at me strangely. "But it's okay. I've since recovered."

My mind is suddenly static, made of the words *THIS WAS A BAD IDEA* laid over and over again until there's no white space left.

I can't see Jason without feeling bad about what I did to Jason. Even if it was the right-ish thing to do.

"I'm sorry," I say.

"I told you I've recovered." He holds out a shopping bag. "I didn't know what to bring, because I was sure you had all the food taken care of. So I brought bubbles."

He doesn't mean champagne. When I look in the bag, I find a dozen plastic bottles of bubble-blowing liquid.

"Everybody loves bubbles, right?" he says.

My mind: Central Park. I blow bubbles in the air. He laughs. A kid on a nearby blanket runs after one that's the size of a pocketbook. An orchestra plays on the Great Lawn.

I am happy.

I am trying to be happy.

I am showing signs of happiness, but I can feel all the effort that goes into that.

I want him to think I am happy.

I don't know what he thinks.

I have no idea which version of the memory is true. The only thing I know for sure is that the little kid chasing after the bubble was definitely happy.

Although it was probably smaller than a pocketbook.

It was.

"Sam?"

Oh no. Concern.

I smile. Cover it all up with a smile. "Sorry. We've had a plumbing issue. It's thrown me a little. Come in."

"Want me to take a look?"

"Sure."

We walk into the kitchen. Stare at the sink.

"I think your drain is clogged," Jason diagnoses.

"Um . . . I know?"

"Do you have any Drano?"

"No. I drank it all."

This is meant to be a joke. Funny. Ha-ha! And maybe if Jason didn't know me, he'd laugh.

He is not laughing.

THIS WAS A BAD IDEA THIS WAS A BAD IDEA THIS WAS A BAD IDEA.

"Why don't we go inside?" I say. "There are some people for you to meet."

BAD IDEA.

Why would I want Jason and Subway Boy to be in the same room? My mind runs through the possible outcomes:

They end up together.

Subway Boy flirts with me and it makes me feel like more of a jerk about Jason.

Subway Boy sees what a bad boyfriend I was with Jason and decides he wants to have nothing to do with me.

They both end up hating me forever.

These are the only outcomes I can think of.

"Or we could stay in the kitchen! The whole night!" I add.

"No. I have a thing or two to say to your sister before the night is through."

"What?"

Jason tries to give me one of those looks that locks from the inside. "I never had a chance with you because I never had a chance of getting your sister's approval. And even though she won in the end, I've always regretted not putting up more of a fight. Your invitation seemed like the perfect opportunity. I mean, in two weeks I'll be moving up to Boston for my internship, and then school. This is my farewell tour. Which means the gloves are off."

Now I'm laughing. Completely bonkers nervous laughter.

"Really," I say, "that's not necessary. Guests are asked to keep their gloves on during a dinner party."

"Everything you've ever done in your life, Sam, has been as an afterthought to what she's done. If she's the strong one, you get to be the weak one—and that, in your mind, absolves you of any responsibility over your own life. She gets away with it, and you get away with it, and the rest of us are just guilty bystanders."

"SO WHAT?" I yell. I yank open a drawer and put my hand inside. "If you want, why don't you just slam this drawer closed? Why be so indirect with the pain you want to inflict— why not just make me *feel it*."

I don't know what I'm doing or saying. I don't know if I want him to slam this drawer closed or if I am being as melodramatic as I always accuse Ilsa of being.

"Come on," Jason says gently. He reaches over and takes my hand out of the drawer. Before it can actually feel like he's holding my hand, I pull away.

"Don't try to help," I tell him. "Don't try to fix things. Just be a guest. Be a polite, friendly guest. Parker's here, and some other people. Go mingle."

"Did your sister know you were inviting Parker?"

"Nope. Surprise!"

"This I gotta see."

He doesn't ask me if I'm going to leave the kitchen with him; he just assumes I will. Which is smart, because if he'd asked, I probably would have said no.

"Here," I tell him. "Carry something in for me."

"You mean the chopped vegetables over here?"

"*Liberté. Fraternité. Crudité.*"

"Well, at least we have one of the three in this apartment."

We head into the living room, and I turn a blind eye to the fact that Parker is already at Czarina's bar, acquainting himself with her vodka.

"Oh, wonderful," KK moans. "Rabbit food, delivered by the Mad Hatter and his teapot."

"Horrible to see you, too, KK," Jason says, putting down the tray.

"Where's Ilsa?" I ask.

"Changing," Parker answers.

KK snorts. "That'll be the day. That leopard has permanent spots."

Subway Boy walks over to Jason, extends his hand, and introduces himself. Jason shakes the hand, introduces himself back. Before this can move on to a second sentence, I jump in and say, "Oh, and you have to meet Frederyk and Caspian."

The two of them step forward, and Caspian extends a pinkie.

"Very funny," Jason says. Then he reaches over and shakes Caspian as if he were a hand.

Frederyk's mouth remains closed, but Caspian screams: "Get off of me! You're *smothering* me!"

KK roars with laughter. Li looks awkward, perhaps because her French maid outfit looks French Canadian next to KK's. Parker holds a glass up to me in offering. Jason lets go of Caspian instantly.

"I'm so sorry," Jason says.

"You just grabbed *his face!*" KK roars. "What kind of monster are you?"

Frederyk has to reach over and straighten Caspian so he is back in order. Both of them look aggrieved.

It's only once his mouth is back in its proper place that Caspian says, "Apology accepted."

Subway Boy smoothly steps in to change the subject. Unfortunately, he does this by turning to Jason and asking, "So how do you know Sam and Ilsa?"

"Oh, Sam broke my heart and Ilsa gave him the hammer to do it with. How about you?"

Subway Boy blinks. "We've traveled together."

Li steps forward to get a celery stick.

"What did I tell you?" KK snaps. "Not within ten feet!"

KK, of course, lives just upstairs. It would be easy enough for her to change. She's so rich she could probably text her closet to prepare a new outfit before she even gets there.

Li looks both miserable and murderous.

"This is going so well!" Parker chirps. "Aren't parties at

Sam and Ilsa's such a blast? Especially when KK is around to spread good cheer!"

"Honey, it's not me, it's *you!*" KK shoots back.

"If you're going to be a bitch, at least find some new material. Nobody loves an unclever bitch. You have to elevate your meanness with the creativity of your phrasing. Otherwise, you're just bitter."

"Yawn, yawn, yawn," KK replies.

Save me, I think. And then I broadcast it. SAVE ME. SAVE ME. SAVE ME.

I'm aiming it at Parker, because that's where my instinct leads me. But he's offering to make Li a drink and complimenting her on her dress, deliberately calling it a dress, I'm sure, to make her feel better.

My SAVE ME veers then, and as it curves toward Jason, I pull it back a little, and it lands instead on Subway Boy. He recognizes it, and I can recognize him recognizing it. Instead of letting it fully connect, I turn away. I can't ask him to save me. He isn't under any obligation.

"I have chips," I mumble to no one in particular. "I'll go get them."

But instead of heading to the kitchen, I head in the direction of the guest room. The door is closed.

Like always, I knock.

"Don't rush me, jerk!" Ilsa hollers. Two seconds later, she throws open the door. For a nanosecond, I see a genuine thrill in her eye. Then she drowns it.

"Who did you think was knocking?" I ask.

"The Secret Service."

"What's going on?" I look down. "And why are you wearing the cat dress? You didn't tell me there were going to be costume changes tonight. I haven't worked them into the run of show."

"I was just feeling feline. Can't a girl get her purr on if she wants to?"

"Parker asked you to wear that, didn't he?"

"I don't know what you're talking about."

"He's always been your catnip. I thought you'd built up some immunity. Clearly not."

"Shut up and zip me."

I step into the room and do so. I feel it's my brotherly obligation to point out that her earrings are now all wrong, and that she better resist the urge to wear cat-print shoes, since that would cross the line between *fancy* and *Cat Fancy*. Our invitation definitely requested the former, not the latter.

"You better be careful when you say that—they can hear you," Ilsa warns. I wonder at first if she means our guests. Then I realize she means the cats on her dress. "They come to life when you're sleeping. And they have claws."

"And thank you for tonight's nightmare!" I chirp.

"By the way, what are you doing here? Why'd you leave the party?"

"To help you with your dress, clearly."

"Evasion! Let's try this again. Why'd you leave the party?"

"Because Jason is here. And he's already established

"Parker, my sister needs help with her dress," I say.

Parker's eyebrow rises. "Is that a request or an order?"

"It's an orquest. A reqder."

He picks up his drink. "I think I'll be needing this where I'm going." Then he heads down the hall.

"Fool," Jason mutters.

"Thus spoke the pot of the kettle," KK observes.

"Ahem." It's Caspian who clears his throat. "Can I help you get the chips?"

"Can you even *eat*?" KK asks.

"Sure." I say this to Frederyk, but he gestures down to Caspian, so I direct my next words to the sock. "This way."

We head into the kitchen. I find a bag of Kettle Chips in the pantry. Caspian, meanwhile, is taking a look at the sink.

"If you have a wrench, I can fix this," he says.

"Which one is a wrench?" I reply. Caspian stares at me unnervingly. "It's a joke," I explain. I retrieve the tool kit from the laundry room . . . but don't know whether to put the wrench in Caspian's mouth or Frederyk's other hand. I'm too scared to do the wrong thing, so I just set the whole box down next to the sink.

"Just one thing before I start," Caspian says. "I know why your sister brought me here—but I just want to confirm it."

"Okay," I say. I honestly have no idea why Ilsa invited him.

"Be honest with me—she wants to set me up with her friend, doesn't she?"

Her friend.

For a minute, I don't get it. Then I hear the buzz saw of her

seven

ILSA

I remember it like it was yesterday: the first dinner party that Czarina allowed Sam and me to attend. We were eight. In the weeks before the party, Czarina relentlessly schooled us on proper etiquette:

1. Don't invite only people who already know each other. Choose guests from different backgrounds, and preferably include someone who's a little bit bigoted in some way but doesn't know it, to keep conversation lively. Mix it up.
2. Make each guest feel welcome, and like they're the most delightful person in the room, even if that means being insincere.
3. Serve delicious food, but don't reach too high trying to create culinary masterpieces. Go with

classics you know will be hits. This is not the time
to try to make a soufflé.
4. If the dinner is terrible, all is not lost. Wine fills
the well of disappointment.
5. Keep your guests' drinks topped off. ALWAYS.
6. Dessert is the most important course. DON'T
MESS THAT UP.

It's clear to me now what Czarina's education neglected.

1. How to talk to a sock puppet.
2. How to feed a sock puppet.
3. How not to laugh in the face of a sock puppet.

Yet, Caspian would do Czarina proud as a guest. To everyone's surprise except his, Caspian turns out to be the life of
the party.

When Li Zhang emerges from Czarina's bedroom wearing
one of Czarina's "schmattes"—a long, loose housedress that
looks like an eggplant-colored muumuu—Caspian admiringly
tells her, "Purple becomes you."

Li Zhang blushes. "Thank you! And you were right. I do
feel a lot more comfortable now that I've changed." She glares
at KK, sipping a martini triumphantly.

I'm pretty sure Caspian made the suggestion for Li Zhang
to change into something of Czarina's so KK could have ex-
clusive maid-uniform rights, not so Li Zhang would feel more
comfortable, but it was a win-win suggestion, so who cares.

I'm not sure what I'm more mesmerized by—Caspian or Johan's Dolly Parton action figures—when I realize that one of the Dollys has a scruffy mutt by her side, with long legs and a spot over one eye, like a patch. "Who's that supposed to be?" I ask Johan, pointing at Dolly and her dog.

Johan says, "I call him Cracker Jack."

"You gave him a name?" I ask, impressed.

Caspian sings from a Dolly song, *"He wasn't much to look at / But he looked alright to me,"* and his pitch is so perfect, and beautiful, that everyone claps.

Then Parker reaches over Caspian to grab some pretzels from a bowl on the coffee table, around which everyone is gathered, waiting for Sam to serve the meal (dinner is taking forever!), and quickly the sweet song moment goes sour. In his eager reaching, Parker accidentally bumps Caspian's . . . er . . . sock, and Caspian apparently doesn't like to be touched. Caspian lets out a small shrieking noise that sounds like a bird being squashed by a tennis ball (served by Serena Williams). The shriek is sharp, piercing, and awful; there's nothing Dolly-like about this noise of Caspian's *at all.* The surprise chirp of horror causes Parker to jump for a moment, and nudge Jason's elbow, which then causes a splash from Jason's drink to land directly on KK's very exposed cleavage. KK slaps Jason, and then Parker, but Caspian saves the day by exclaiming, "It's not him, it's me!"

Everyone laughs—even Parker, who Sam has told me hates this joke.

KK looks at Caspian and then shoots me a look like, *Who*

is *this guy? Not* like, *Who is this nutjob?* but more like, *Where has this guy been all my life?*

When KK and I were scamming on hot guys playing basketball in Central Park, and our eyes landed on pale but beautiful, blond Freddie, we honestly had no idea about Freddie's friend Caspian. I guess Caspian naps when Freddie's hands are otherwise busy? We totally believed Freddie's story about him being an exchange student from Poland. His English was stunted and accented, he was wearing a white T-shirt that said SOLIDARNOść in red, and he drank a cold-pressed beet juice to cool off during time-outs. He had the awkward but resigned dribble of a player groomed in a formerly Communist country. Seemed plausibly Polish to us. Freddie should have been excellent Sam-bait. Eastern European accent: check. Sporty-looking but poorly sport-playing: check. Bleeding-heart lefty: check. Healthy-juice drinker: check.

Fooled us.

Caspian? He has a flawless American accent (sounds like New Orleans or New Jersey, which are pretty much the same accent, according to Czarina), and his English is perfectly fluent, if not downright native. By the way he stares at KK's cleavage, he's definitely not gay. Freddie's blue eyes are stone cold and unmoving, but if it was possible for drool to form from Caspian's pert little red-stitched mouth as his green button eyes ogle KK's maid outfit, it would.

Caspian's charm is short-lived, however. In my direction, he exclaims, "Geraldine, I see you and your deformity! I *despise* you!"

Everyone looks at me. Clearly, he's talking to me, but I don't get it. "Who's Geraldine?" I ask Caspian. I'm slightly wishing that Geraldine is another sock puppet. I'm feeling sad for Czarina. So many dinner parties she threw in this apartment, and here's the most interesting guest of all time at the end of this apartment's tenure in our family, and Czarina's not here to meet him.

Like it's obvious, Caspian says, "The blue cat on your dress."

I point out, "There are several blue cats on my dress. It's a pattern."

"Geraldine!" Caspian spews. "The one with the lazy eye! She *disgusts* me."

And there it is. Our bigot: check. Czarina would be so happy.

There's a palpable pause from the other guests, as I believe we're all trying to figure out exactly where that line is between eccentric and lunatic, and should we be amused or scared? Sam arrives from the kitchen, sweaty and disheveled, before we make the official determination. He carries the lasagna to the dinner table and pronounces, "Time to eat. Sorry it's late. The sink thing threw me off. Thanks for the wrench save, Caspian." We gather around the table and inspect Sam's creation. It looks crisp, steaming, with browned, gurgling cheese on the top. Sam adds, "It's a little overbaked. Sorry."

I'm pleased. Jason Goldstein-Chung loves Sam's lasagna, and tonight, he won't get to enjoy it at all. If we're lucky, it will burn his mouth and give him indigestion. Jason was never good enough for Sam, or Sam's lasagna.

Parker pats Sam's back supportively. "Looks delicious," Parker says.

The salad is already on the table, and Caspian leans over to inspect it. There's no scrunching of his nose (because he doesn't have one), but he lets out an audible sniffing sound despite Freddie's nose and mouth both not moving. Caspian says, "Is that . . . mayonnaise I smell in the salad?"

Of course we're all wondering how Caspian actually has a sense of smell, but gentleman Sam answers Caspian straightforwardly. "In the dressing," Sam says. "It's a Waldorf salad."

"Why don't you just pile a can of lard directly on the lettuce greens while you're at it?" Caspian spews.

"Hey!" I start to say, about to put Caspian in his place. Why'd he get so suddenly bratty? Low blood sugar? Skipped his meds today? Then I remember he's a sock puppet. Somehow it seems exactly right that he should be so inconsistent with his moods.

KK's already on her phone. "Just ordered a sushi platter."

Li Zhang says, "Should we order a pizza? I mean, in addition to that amazing-looking lasagna?" Her face reveals total revulsion to Sam's cooking. I don't know why he's so off tonight. Usually his meals are masterpieces. I pray the anxiety that Sam tries so hard to suffocate by not acknowledging it exists is not the chef really in charge of Sam's soul—and culinary prowess—tonight.

Sam sighs. I sigh. I'll fucking kill anyone who dares to order in more food. (I can't do anything about KK, and the sushi platter will make her less whiny. But everyone else better g-damn love my brother's lasagna.)

Always knowing my feelings before I speak them, and sounding like the tallest and strongest and deepest-voiced man in the room that he is, Parker intones, "We will love this lasagna. And we will love it hard."

I try not to look at him. I don't want Parker to sense how fast my heart is beating. I set my expression to my best poker face.

Johan hums the tune, *And I / will always love you.*

We've barely sat down at the dinner table when the doorbell rings. KK runs to the door, expecting her sushi platter. But the newest guest is one we didn't invite. It's Madeleine Hogue, the seven-year-old daughter of the family next door, my favorite babysitting charge. She runs into the living room holding out a plate of cookies. "Here, Ilsa! Cook and I made your favorite cookies for your last party!" Maddy has a maid, a nanny from Paraguay to help her with her Spanish, a family chef, and a personal Pilates instructor at her disposal. She's livin' *la buena vida* here at the Stanwyck.

I take a whiff of the most sincerely sinful cookies in the history of the world. It's a recipe I saw in *People* magazine once at the dentist's office, and Dr. Segal would not approve of its ingredients (or maybe she would, in the interest of keeping her business afloat). They're called Junk in da Trunk cookies, and they're like chocolate chip cookies, but with butterscotch morsels, malted milk balls, peanuts, potato chips, and pretzels added in. If I were a scientist, I'd run a study to find out if there was ever a more delicious cookie recipe invented that could be worse for your health. Maddy knows they're my favorites.

"Thank you, my darling Maddy," I say. I place the cookies on the coffee table and return to my dining chair, and hold out my arms for Maddy to jump onto my lap.

She takes her usual seat and I introduce her to the gang that don't already know her. "Everybody, this is Maddy. She lives next door. Her parents bought this apartment and they're going to knock through those living room walls to combine their unit with this one. Maddy, this is everybody."

In a few months, after the renovation, Maddy's sweet, privileged life will be even better, because her nanny is going back to Paraguay, and I am going to take the nanny's place. I am going to live in Czarina's guest room when it becomes Maddy's nanny's room. It will be my own. Maddy knows not to tell our little secret, though. I wanted to wait until after the last dinner party, until a few weeks after Czarina has moved out, before announcing my new job to Sam and the rest of the family. We haven't even begun sitting shiva for the apartment. The timing is still too delicate. They all still think I'm leaving for Quinnipiwherever at the end of the summer.

"Hi, Maddy," everyone says, except KK, who snaps, "I thought you were the sushi, dummy." Maddy giggles. She knows better than to be offended by KK.

Maddy tells Sam, "Your lasagna looks amazing, as always." My sweetest liar. My best protégé. "And cook made an extra batch of cookies for you to bring home to your parents." I look at Maddy proudly. My protégé learned these excellent cookie manners from me.

"They're in Vegas for the weekend. LiberaceCon," Parker jokes. "Can I take them home to mine?"

"Sure!" says Maddy.

"Those cookies will make you fat, Maddy," snipes Caspian, which is totally unfair. Maddy is a little bit pudgy but so much less since her parents put the Pilates instructor on retainer.

"Don't be a dick, Caspian," Jason says to Caspian.

Maddy looks at Jason, then at me. "He said 'dick,'" she whispers. Then she glances at Caspian, and takes in the situation. There's a sock puppet at our dinner table. "Who's *he*?" she asks.

"Your worst nightmare," says Caspian, completely serious, and then, in a baby voice, he adds, "Widdle Maddy poo-poo."

Johan stands up. "I've had it with you." Before Freddie can realize his intent, Johan grabs the sock off Freddie's hand. "You're excused for the evening, Caspian."

Johan heads to the back of the apartment. "Where are you going?" Freddie cries out, with all the anguish of his arm just having been amputated without anesthetic.

Freddie rushes behind Johan, who takes off in a sprint, calling out, "This *domkop* is going down the *privaat*."

I don't speak Afrikaans, but I'm pretty sure poor Caspian is about to meet his end in Czarina's toilet.

What a clog that will be.

Poor Caspian.

eight

SAM

As much as you obsess about all the things that can go wrong, it is inevitably something you can't imagine that ends up going wrong. Which justifies worrying about *everything*, just to make sure it's all covered.

Johan's disadvantaged because he has no idea where the bathroom is. That momentary pause—looking at the doors, trying to figure out which one holds the porcelain throne—gives Frederyk enough time to go for the tackle. I am about five steps behind as he lunges—Johan tries to dodge, but he's not quick enough. They both go tumbling down.

"Stop it, guys!" I yell. "Seriously, stop it."

I expect Frederyk to grab for Caspian, but instead he's trying to get Johan's wrist in a choke hold, so Johan will let go. Then I realize this makes sense—in any tug of war, Caspian's going to lose.

"STOP!" I say, louder. But no one is listening to me. I switch tactics and yell, "JOHAN!"

Now he hears me. He looks in my direction, and Frederyk takes this moment to get in a blow to Johan's stomach.

"No!" I call out, and before I know what I'm doing, I'm standing over both of them, pulling them apart. Frederyk regains his senses and recoils. Johan remains sweaty and disheveled beneath me, Caspian still scrunched in his hand.

"Give him to me," I say.

Subway Boy shakes his head, and he's not really Subway Boy anymore. He's this stranger in my apartment. Which makes me sad.

He says, "I was fine indulging his . . . whim while the sock was being pleasant. But not if he's just going to use it as a mouthpiece for meanness. We have enough of that from actual human beings nowadays."

I look over to Frederyk to see what his response will be. He just holds out his hand—not the Caspian hand, the other hand—imploring.

"You have to give him back," I insist. "I'm sure he'll behave better now."

"Whose side are you on?" Johan asks.

And I say, plainly, "In this case, his."

"Fine."

He hands over Caspian as if it's the only gift he's ever going to give me. I offer him my free hand, but he stands up on his own.

"I was only trying to help," he tells me. "I thought you'd appreciate that."

"I do," I say. "It's just that Frederyk—"

"—is crazy?"

"That's not nice."

"Okay, *Mum*. I'm sorry. Shall I go?"

No.

No—

I—

"No! I want you here."

"I guess I'll go back to the table, then. You can stay here and preside over the tearful reunion."

If Ilsa were saying this—or, God forbid, KK—the words would be corrosive, combative beasts. But the way Johan says it—he's hurt. I'm not the only Subway Boy who realizes things have derailed.

I try to think of a Parton song to bring him back, but my thoughts are more Dalí than Dolly at the moment.

"I'll be there in a sec," I say.

"Okay," he replies. Then he leaves me in the hall, Caspian in my hand.

"Here," I say to Frederyk. He takes the sock from me and puts it back where it belongs.

"Thank you," Caspian says quietly.

Frederyk looks like he's prepared for me to be angry, for me to lash out at him for ruining everything. Which maybe he has. But maybe if it could be ruined this easily, it wasn't worth having, anyway. I don't know.

"It's okay," I tell him—Frederyk, not Caspian.

"That was very close," Caspian observes. Frederyk nods.

I am still looking Frederyk in the eye. "You have to be nicer," I say. "You can't just shoot his mouth off. I'm not saying what Johan did was right—but you have to know that we all wanted to do it. Except maybe KK."

At the mention of her name, Frederyk blushes and looks away.

"No," I say. "You can't possibly like *KK*."

Neither Frederyk nor Caspian denies it.

I press on. "And did you think the way to her heart was through her spleen? Were you being obnoxious to *impress* her?!"

Caspian nods.

"Bad strategy?" he asks.

"For the rest of us, absolutely. For KK—probably worse. She doesn't want some amateur version of her. This is New York—there are plenty of guys who fit that bill. KK's not-very-deep, not-very-dark secret is that she finds her routine as tedious as the rest of us do. When you think you're the most interesting person in the room, you're never interested in anything else. So your best shot—your only shot, really—is to be even more interesting than she is. You were doing well until you stooped to her level."

"I really messed it up, didn't I?"

"Not necessarily. She hasn't left yet."

"I mean for you. I really messed it up for you."

The hurt look on Johan's face surfaces in my mind, and I try to shove it away.

"It'll be fine," I say. But everyone in the hallway knows how empty those words can be.

Caspian can't look me in the eye. He's just staring at the ground. And then I realize . . . Frederyk has put his hand down.

"I appreciate you taking my side," he—Frederyk—says. And in an instant, I see how hard it is for him to say it.

"It's okay," I tell him. Then I reach out, take Caspian by the chin, and move him so he's looking me in the eye, too. "I don't know exactly what it's like, but . . . I know what it's like. Our tribe has to stand up for one another, right? Because there are plenty of people who don't know what it's like at all."

I have already done so many things wrong tonight. But this, finally, feels like something right. There isn't anything more to say.

"Let's go back," I tell them.

Ilsa's laying down of the law must have worked—or maybe people are so afraid of conversation at this point that the lasagna seems the better option for their mouths. Whatever the case, dinner's well under way, and is being consumed with gusto.

"Where's Maddy?" I ask.

"A hawk came in the window and carried her away," KK replies.

"But don't worry," Parker quickly adds. "We still have the cookies."

I look over to Johan, who turns away the second I make eye contact. Then I look to Ilsa, who's seen the whole thing.

"Here," she says, passing over the lasagna. "Don't be one of those hosts who doesn't have a chance to eat."

I sit down. Frederyk, who followed me in, remains standing.

"Excuse me," Caspian says. "May I have everyone's attention?"

"By all means!" KK trills. "The sock has the floor!"

Frederyk takes a deep breath, then Caspian continues.

"I did not mean to disrupt this party, or to scare away the cookie-bearing girl. This is the first time I have been invited to such a dinner, and in trying to figure out how to behave, I behaved the wrong way. I understand this now, and it will not occur again."

"Please sit down," Ilsa says. "These things happen all the time."

Both Parker and Jason raise their eyebrows at that . . . but neither says a word.

"Here." KK takes Frederyk's plate and puts some sushi on it. Then, as an afterthought, she separates one of the rolls off to the side—for Caspian, presumably.

"Thank you," Caspian mutters. Frederyk sits down.

KK launches into a monologue on how she had to try at least *a dozen* sushi chefs before she could find *one* that could deliver a decent California roll after midnight, California time. I find it hard to imagine something I care less about, but it does give the rest of us an opportunity to dig in without bearing any of the weight of the conversation.

When she's done, it's Jason who picks up the mantle.

"This is really good," he says, gesturing to the lasagna with his fork. "Thank you, Ilsa."

Ilsa looks momentarily confused. "You know I had nothing to do with the lasagna, Jason," she says.

"And the salad! You've perfected your recipe, Ilsa."

She eyes him wearily.

"You're teasing me—is that it? It happens that Sam is an excellent cook. There's no need for me to contribute."

"Oh, but you always manage to *contribute*, don't you? There isn't a situation, big or small, that doesn't require the contribution of your opinion. Sam's cooking, Sam's boyfriends, Sam's future, Sam's life—your opinion is the only ingredient you can provide, isn't it? Just a little dash of poison for any occasion."

I jump in. "Jason. This is not why I invited you."

Ilsa waves me off. "No, it's okay. It's been months since Jason's graced us with his presence—but how refreshing to know he's still an expert on your life and family!"

"It's all about figuring out the patterns. People like you are sudoku for armchair therapists."

"Fuck you, she's a Sunday crossword," KK contributes. Then she adds, "I happen to be very good at crosswords."

There's a booming noise from outside that shushes everyone.

"Was that thunder?" Jason asks.

"Or was it a bomb?" Parker says.

He's not joking.

There's another sonic burst.

"Like God clearing his throat," Li says.

A torrent of rain is unleashed. Our windows are open, and the wind blows through, making the tablecloth a ghost about to lift.

"It's just a summer storm," Ilsa says. "That's all." I stand up to close the window, but Ilsa tells me, "No, don't. I like it like this."

I'm worried about the rain coming in, about rugs getting wet, wood getting warped. But I don't want everyone to know the extent of my agitation. I want to cover it up. So I sit down.

"It's only a matter of time before the city drowns," Li says.

"Excuse me?" KK seems personally offended by this fact.

"I don't mean tonight. Or even in the next few years. But eventually, the oceans will rise, and everyone in this city will need to find a new place to live. I've seen it."

"You've seen it?" Jason says.

"I know it sounds strange, but I've always been a little bit of an oracle. Or at least I've had oracular dreams for as long as I can remember. After Hurricane Sandy, this one became more pronounced. Seeing the water rise in the streets. Everyone forced to evacuate. It always makes me so sad. And angry, too."

"Well, thank God I live on the top floor!" KK chirps.

"And where do you think all of the electricity and drainage and water for that apartment comes from—the air?" Parker asks.

I shudder.

"I'm not saying this to be scary," Li continues. "I just don't see any point in ignoring the inevitable. If we talk about it, at least we have a chance of navigating it."

"I wish that's how it worked," I say. I don't mean to say it. That is, I don't mean to say it to anyone but myself. But I've said it out loud.

"What do you mean?" Johan asks.

"It's nothing," I say. "Never mind."

"No," Ilsa says. "Tell us."

You're trapping me, I think. But I don't say that out loud. They're all looking at me.

I—

I—

"I'm just not sure talking about things makes any difference. I mean, when something's worrying me, I think about it and I think about it and I think about it, and I don't know that any of the words I think change the situation at all. I just get lost in it more."

"I'm not talking about *thinking*," Li says. "I'm talking about *talking*."

"What's the difference?" I ask.

It's Caspian who answers. "The difference is that when you're talking, there's usually someone else in the room, and the hope is that the other person can help you understand it more. Or you can help each other understand it more."

"I grew up in a house where there was a lot of thinking and not much talking," Johan says. "Believe me, there's a difference."

"Well, I grew up in an apartment where there was a whole

lot of talking and not much thinking," Jason says. "At least, not until the divorce. And, let me tell you, that's no fun, either."

Ilsa's attention is still on Li.

"Do you think there's hope?" she asks. "I mean, for the future."

And maybe it's Czarina's caftan, or maybe it's just the eerie wind rushing around us, but as she prepares her response, Li truly does look oracular.

"Of course there's hope," she says. "There's always hope. We have an endless capacity for hope. We just tend to lock that capacity down."

"So we're not just rearranging deck chairs on the *Titanic*?" Parker asks.

"Wrong question," Li replies. "My point isn't about deck chairs. Nobody cares about the deck chairs. What I'm saying is—there comes a time, long before the accident, when you decide how many lifeboats the *Titanic* should have. That's what we need to do—in many ways, it's the only thing we *can* do. Make sure we have plenty of lifeboats."

Is this why I'm so scared of what comes next? When I stay here for college, Ilsa will be the only lifeboat left with me. And she leaks. She doesn't mean to, but she leaks when I weigh too heavily on her. I need more lifeboats. But at the same time, many of my lifeboats are in this room right now, and I'm still scared. I really wish my mind would stop being such a contradictory jerk to me. Because how can I feel that the future is way too big for me to change it and at the same time feel that if I make the smallest wrong move, I'm going to cause permanent damage?

"Can you see specifics about the future, too?" Caspian asks Li.

"There's a difference between an oracle and a fortune-teller," she replies. "Sorry."

Caspian shakes his head. "No, no, no—I don't want to know my future."

"I imagine it all goes down the tubes," KK informs the sock. "You should've known that from the moment you were knit."

"There's no need for that," I tell her.

KK laughs. "Since when did you become such a defender of footwear?"

"Caspian is *not a sock*."

"What is he, then? An oracle, too?"

"Caspian is CASPIAN." I have no idea why I'm shouting at her. "And if you're not going to treat him like everyone else, you can go back up to your own apartment and order all the sushi you want."

KK's eyes sparkle. "But I *am* treating him like I treat everyone else, don't you see?"

Ilsa, of course, backs her up. "She has a point."

Jason sighs theatrically, looks at KK, and says, "You're awful." Then he turns to Ilsa and says, "You're not much better."

"Stop," I tell him.

"Why are you defending her?" he replies.

There have to be thousands of answers. I just can't think of one at the moment.

But it's not like I even have a chance.

"Why are you still in love with him?" Ilsa accuses.

"Ilsa," Parker says in a voice you'd use with a bear that's picked up a toddler.

"I really like the lasagna."

At first, I don't even know who's spoken. Then I realize it's Johan.

He goes on.

"When I was a kid, my mom did this thing with lasagna— she would use alphabetic noodles to spell out messages for us, usually in the bottom layer. So we had to eat it very, very carefully. Usually we'd be rushing through dinner—I have four brothers—but when it was lasagna, you would have thought we were excavating a dinosaur. Sometimes she'd make it so each of us got a word, and we'd have to wait until everyone was finished to see what the sentence was. You have to keep in mind—this was a totally rigid household. Everything was run with military precision. So when our mom would do this, it was almost like . . . I don't know. Like there was an under-ground. A rebellion. So, you know, I can't eat lasagna without thinking of that."

I have no idea why he's telling us this. And then I realize he's telling us this to shut everyone else up. And I feel . . . grateful.

"My mother did that with sushi," KK chimes in. "She'd have the sushi chef write messages with soy sauce on the inside of the seaweed wraps. Things like *Eat the rich* and *Die banker die*. Come to think of it, maybe it wasn't my mother telling him to write those things. I'm kidding, of course."

When none of us laugh, KK sticks her tongue out. Then she says, "Fine. Be that way. In the meantime, I believe my dear friend Ilsa has a big announcement she wants to make. . . ."

nine

ILSA

Poor, sweet Sam. He's the only emotionally stable person at the table. Or, as usual, he's trying too hard to be.

KK smells blood. She gets like this. When there's the chance for a massacre, she immediately wants more, before the knives have even officially come out, or before the sock puppet gets flushed down the toilet. She needs an infusion of rapidly escalating high stakes that result in complete carnage, jam-packed within a short period of time. She watches too much Shondaland and *Game of Thrones*. Forgive her.

She wants me to make the announcement about my new living situation so she can witness the fallout: Sam wailing about me moving into his beloved room at Czarina's, and then him losing it at me for keeping my plans secret for so long. Jason G-C gloating that I am in my beloved brother's bad graces. Parker betrayed that I would unsettle his best friend.

Johan hastily putting his Dollygurines back in his violin case before they're used as battle props. Li Zhang stress-eating the entire lemon tart Sam prepared for dessert.

I'm not playing KK's game. I evolve at staring-at-a-crackling-fire-on-the-TV-monitor pace. I'll tell Sam when I'm ready, not when KK is ready.

But I do have an announcement. "Time to lock up the phones." I should have done this as people arrived. The storm is getting bigger outside Czarina's epic-view windows, and I can already see how the rest of the night will go. It will be lost to Instagram postings of lightning over Manhattan's skyline and gales falling on the unlucky people in view down on the sidewalk. Or worse, snaps of Sam's woeful lasagna. Better to remove the phones entirely. That might be the best we can salvage from this meal.

"Refuse," says KK. "Absolutely not."

I stand up and grab her phone out of her hand before she can move it from my reach. "I love you so much, KK." I place a kiss on top of her head. I know I'm the only person who finds her adorable, but someone's got to, dear neglected bankers' daughter.

Czarina insists that no one have their phone at the table when she invites the family to dinner. I follow her lead and retrieve from the foyer the small lockbox she keeps for phones. I return to the dining table and circle around it with the open box for our guests to deposit their phones in. I place KK's in there first.

"Could you give me a better one when we get these back?" Johan asks, dropping his in. "Mine's about five years old."

"Jason will volunteer to give you his, I'm sure," I say.

I glare at Jason. He return-glares at me, but deposits the latest iPhone into the box. Jason is the kind of guy who lines up at the Apple store the night before the tech behemoth puts its latest phone on the market, and then posts about it all night and morning like he's competing in a triathlon instead of slumping down on pavement literally doing nothing.

When I reach Caspian, he says, "I don't have a phone."

"Because you don't have the finger dexterity to type texts?" Jason asks. Such a snob. As a child, Jason once won the Fastest Text Typer at a county fair. Because that's the kind of county fair he asked to be taken to as a kid.

"Because I prefer to communicate in person!" says Caspian. Freddie tosses his phone into the box, though.

After I've collected the remaining phones, I lock the box and return it to the foyer.

"Time for dessert?" Sam asks.

"Time for Czarina's champagne collection," says KK.

"Seconded," says Parker.

Sam goes toward the kitchen, while I lead the group into the living room as thunder rumbles outside like God is juggling boulders in the sky and threatening to slam them down onto Manhattan in one apocalyptic seizure.

Li Zhang pales as the rumble gets louder. "Thunder terrifies me."

I sit her down on Czarina's most comfortable chair not facing the window. "Sam will play piano for us after dessert. That will drown out the noise." I'm remembering a birthday dinner at Czarina's when Sam and I turned ten. He was just starting to get good on the piano. There was a terrifying thunderstorm going on outside. Sam sat down at the piano to soothe everyone's nerves. I couldn't stand the attention his music playing was getting, so I started doing cartwheels and handsprings around the piano. I had a poor landing on one, shaking the floor so hard, it caused the fallboard—which covers the keys when the piano isn't in use—to come down hard onto Sam's fingers. He honestly was not that hurt—maybe there was a bruised fingernail—but I got sent to Czarina's room as punishment for the duration of the party. No cake for Ilsa.

I'll behave better this time.

Parker says, "The sweetest sound ever; you'll love it." I give him a look, to test if our psychic connection still works. It does! He sits down on the floor by Li Zhang, to make her feel reassured in the storm, which I'd like all my guests except Jason to feel.

"Who wants coffee? Who wants tea?" Jason asks the group. He turns to me. "You're supposed to offer these to your guests, Ilsa."

KK reaches over to Czarina's lacquer china cabinet. "Nobody cares about tea, Jason."

"I wouldn't mind some tea," says Johan.

I say, "Find Sam in the kitchen. He'll show you where the tea is." I should bring him the tea myself, of course. I'm a terrible hostess, I know. I hope Johan doesn't post Yelp reviews. But I'm fickle. Johan's lost his status as my favorite guest (hello, Caspian). Johan can get his own damn tea.

KK pulls out the one full bottle of brandy that we haven't topped off with water since previous dinner parties. "Now we have a party," says KK. She takes out Czarina's brandy glasses and places them on the coffee table in front of the long sofa, where Jason and Freddie have sat down, Jason on one end, and Caspian idling upright over Freddie's elbow on the sofa's arm at the other end. "Who's in?" she asks, about to pour.

My hand goes up, along with those of Parker, Li Zhang, and Caspian, who bobs up and down. "Single shot or double shot?" KK asks Freddie/Caspian.

"Double," says Caspian.

While she's pouring, Sam enters the living room. "Ta-da!" he announces. He places the lemon tart on the other end of the coffee table for everyone to admire. "Lemon tart for dessert."

"It's green!" cries out Caspian. "Are you sure it's not a lime tart?"

Sam appears crestfallen. "The lemons at Fairway weren't that great when I went shopping this morning. But I didn't think it looked that bad."

"It looks *amazing*," says Parker, giving everyone else The Look.

The tart doesn't look green, in all fairness. But it doesn't look exactly lemony, either, in all honesty.

"So good," Li Zhang affirms.

"Yummy," I say.

"Can't wait," says Jason.

"Allergic," pipes in Caspian.

"Nah," says KK.

All of a sudden, a bloodcurdling bolt of lightning cracks across the sky. Caspian lets out his signature shriek. Li Zhang looks terrified. "That was nothing," says Parker, trying to keep the mood calm.

But it wasn't nothing. Because then the power goes out. We're left sitting in the living room with no light—and no light coming from the street or other buildings, either. I look out the window: darkness, except for car lights. It's not just our building that's lost power. In that darkness I have a flash vision of what later tonight could be like, if I go downtown with Parker to compete in a dance contest. It's funny; I can't see me going. Not because I don't want to dance with Parker. Because I don't feel the need to prove I can.

Sam immediately goes into Boy Scout mode. "Everyone stay seated till I find Czarina's emergency supply box in the coat closet." I hear him walking toward the foyer, and it's true that he could probably find his way across Czarina's apartment blindfolded—there are no sounds of him bumping any furniture or knocking over glasses or other trinkets. He reaches the foyer and calls out, "Ilsa, what's the combination for Czarina's lockbox? I found a small flashlight, but it's flickering—I think the battery is just about dead. But I can use it to open the lockbox, and then we can use the flashlights on our phones."

"Zero-one-one-eight!" I call out. I see the faintest flicker of light coming from the foyer.

"Our birthday—of course!" Sam calls out. January

eighteenth. "Are you sure that's the number, Ilsa? It's not working."

"I'm sure. Unless Czarina changed it after that dinner where Dad stole his phone back to check the basketball score."

"She must have changed it. Stupid Dad! Why couldn't he just have ignored the game for an hour?"

"It was the March Madness Final Four game!" I remind Sam. "Syracuse was playing."

"You don't mess with a man's phone during that time," Parker intones.

"Agreed," says Caspian or Freddie, I'm not sure which.

"Shit, the flashlight's burned out," says Sam.

"I'm scared," says Li Zhang.

I sit down on the carpet and use the smell of delicious Parker to crawl my way to her other side, my knee knocking against Parker's, making me truly weak in the knees.

"It's okay," I tell Li Zhang. "I'm sure the power will be back on any minute."

The vengeful deity in the sky has other plans. Another lightning bolt flashes, making the previous one look like a practice run, and in that moment of light, I see the abject terror on Li Zhang's face. Parker must see it, too, because he assures Li Zhang, "Don't worry. Ilsa and me, we're right here. We've got you. We're your lifeboats."

Caspian says, "Mother Nature is just letting out some energy. It's like a low-grade earthquake. You know those are good, right? Because they settle the ground enough to hold off the big ones."

was a silent-screen actress when the movie industry was just starting out in New York City, before it moved to California. She always played British high-society ladies."

Sam says, "Although, apparently in real life she had a thick Brooklyn accent. Grew up in Sheepshead Bay."

"That part's true," says KK. "She haunts the hallways crooning"—and here KK uses an old-time Brooklyn accent—"'Who died and made YOU boss, wisenheimer?'"

"Help!" cries out a voice from the kitchen.

"Johan!" says Sam. "I forgot he was in the kitchen. Someone needs to rescue him."

"You do that, Sam the Man," says Parker. And I feel Parker's hand give mine a squeeze. This thing we share. It's either psychic or psychotic, or both. It leaves me breathless.

"Please can we be quiet?" Li Zhang asks. "Until this is over."

"Our voices don't calm you?" Parker asks.

"No. And as much as the thunder noise stresses me, I also like focusing my attention on it. Makes me feel like I am conquering it, rather than the other way around."

"So we will be quiet, then," comes Caspian's voice.

As quiet settles, I understand why she prefers it. The rhythm of the hard-falling rain is almost hypnotic, with none of the usual city noise, like honking horns and yelling people, coming up from below. The power outage and the tenacity of the rain seem to have cleared the street—and the air. Such quiet is a stranger to me—exactly the guest I didn't know we needed. I feel like I can finally think. Assess.

ten

SAM

I am jealous of my eyes.

I am jealous of the way they know how to adjust without me having to tell them to adjust.

I am jealous that the moment after it turns dark, they know how to make the darkness easier to navigate.

I am making my way back to the kitchen to find Johan. I am following the sound of his voice. I am taking step after careful step, and as I do, the darkness seems to second-guess itself. It retreats from completeness and lets a grayness in. I feel a little better, a little more in control.

I am not afraid of the dark. I am afraid of knocking things over in the dark, of hurting myself in the dark, of getting lost in the dark, of being attacked in the dark.

"Hello?" Johan calls out.

"I'll be there in a second," I call back. "Stand away from the door."

I swing it inward. I don't hit him.

"Sam?"

The clock on the oven has gone out. The refrigerator is just another piece of furniture. I remember I left the knives out, but don't remember where.

"I see you," I say. He is the dark patch at the counter. He is the object of my attention even when I can't make out where his clothes end and his skin begins. "I'm here. I'm sorry. You were drowned out in all the hysterics."

There's a pause as still as the darkness. Then he says, "I have a confession to make."

I come closer. "Yes?"

"I may have stayed in here to avoid the hysterics."

"Oh."

"And I may have called for help because I knew you'd be the one to respond."

He is now close enough to be more than an outline. It's like a fairy tale, and we're the shadows who are turning back into boys.

"Of course I'd be the one to respond," I say. "I'm *always* the one who responds."

I'm surprised by how bitter I sound, especially in front of him.

"That does seem to be the dynamic," he says. "From what I've observed."

He's moved his leg out so it's touching the side of my leg. I am trying not to notice this. Instead, I am noticing that he's known me for all of two hours and he already thinks he knows everything about me, and Ilsa, and our lives.

I am also noticing that he's probably right.

"It's just the way we are," I explain. Which isn't an explanation at all, really.

"That's okay. She isn't the one I wanted to walk through the door."

This should be exactly what I want to hear. I should be leaning into this moment, leaning into this boy in the darkness.

But I—

I—

He can't point out what's wrong and then say it's okay, just because he wants to kiss me.

I pull away a little. I become a little less clear in his eyes.

"I wanted to respond," I tell him.

"I know. That's sweet." He stops resting against the counter. He moves closer to me. "You're very sweet."

"No, no—you don't get it. I mean, I *wanted* to respond. It's not that I respond because she won't. It's not like I'm ruled by the dynamic you're talking about. I'd want to do it anyway, even if she weren't there to *not* do it. Does that make sense? Does it make any sense at all? Because I want it to make sense. It feels really important that it make sense, that my caring can be separate from her not caring. If that's even true—because I think she *does* care about a lot of things. I'm just more honest in expressing it."

Oh God, listen to yourself. He doesn't want to hear this!

His hand touches me right below my shoulder. Supportive, or at least attempting to be.

"It's okay," he tells me.

"No," I reply. "That's too easy. It's not helpful."

He puts his hand down. "Give me a chance to talk, okay?"

He hates you, I think. *He totally hates you.*

He goes on. "I understand what you mean—I just dated this guy for almost a year, and it was like he felt we had to be exact complements; if he was bitchy, I had to be a saint; if he was the life of the party, I had to be the death of the party; if he was Mr. Public, I had to be Mr. Private. The stupid thing is, I went along with it. Because I thought, fine, if I was going to be those things anyway, there were plenty of other areas where being complementary was . . . beneficial."

I don't want to hear this. I don't like it when other people are brought into the room. Because then you can't ignore them.

But I can't just stand here, either. He's telling me something. I have to respond.

"So what happened?" I ask. It's the safest thing I can think to say.

"It's so ridiculous."

"It can't be any more ridiculous than our dinner party," I point out.

"True. But this is that mundane ridiculousness where something way too small becomes something way too big. Do you really want to know why we broke up?"

"Yes," I say. With some hesitation, of course. I know it's a bad sign when a guy spends too much time talking about his ex.

Johan sighs. "It was over his phone."

Then he stops. It is unclear to me whether they broke up while talking over the phone, or whether the phone played a more important role. "Go on," I tell him.

I can see Johan reach behind him to find the counter again. Once he finds it, he leans. But we still feel close.

"So, I was at his apartment, hanging out after rehearsal. We were on the couch, watching *Drag Race*. Anyway, we're there, side by side, and it's feeling comfortable. Then he says, 'I need my phone.' And I ask him where it is, and he says it's in his bedroom. Then he asks me to get it. I tell him he can get it himself, and his response is that, no, that's *my* job. He's joking, but he's not really joking, and I can see that this is a game to him—can he make me do it? And I realize that usually the answer is yes, I will do it, so the game can be over quickly. But this time I refuse—and he's *hurt* by it. Genuinely hurt. Why would I refuse such a simple request? 'You like helping me!' he tells me—or something like that. And I say, 'Stan, clearly I don't like it right now.'"

"Stan," I say.

"Yes—and first I thought he was going to make everything right, say he was sorry and get his own damn phone so he could text or tweet or whatever it is he does. But no. Here's the beautiful part. *He calls me selfish.* And I say, 'You, of all people, are not allowed to deploy that adjective.' It goes from there."

It's in the middle of that sentence that the lights come back on. For a moment, we are blinded. Then our eyes adjust.

"A tweeter named Stan," I say.

Johan nods. "Stan Ball. He goes to your school, right?"

"But he . . . he never tweeted about you."

"The only selfless thing he ever did! I said if he made me part of his running commentary, I'd be the one running. And he heeded that. Until we broke up."

The kitchen has come back to life, and is adding its own commentary, blinking and groaning and ticking its way back to reality.

Johan goes on. "I guess he talked about coming here. I didn't make the connection until I showed up."

It shouldn't matter to me that Johan isn't a complete stranger. If anything, it should make me feel better, that we have something in common, even if it's #Stantastic. But instead, it's like he's ruining the story of us, the story of this great random meeting on the subway. It's still random, but it no longer feels *serendipitously* random.

I'm realizing it's pretty quiet in the living room—which could mean either that things have settled down or that the chaos has turned into a black hole.

I can't help it: I wonder if anything in there has been broken. Or is in the process of being broken. Or is about to be broken unless I intercede.

"We should probably see what they're up to," I tell Johan.

He looks disappointed. Or confused. Or annoyed.

I guess the point is that I can't tell which.

I guess the point is that I can't adjust.

I guess the point is that, yes, I am always the one to

respond. But that's no guarantee that the response will be the right one.

All I'm good at, it seems, is showing up. And even that's a challenge—like when Johan and I get back to the living room and find a strangely silent disarray. Frederyk and KK are uncomfortably sharing a love seat. Li has her eyes closed and is breathing deeply. Parker looks amused. Jason looks unamused. And Ilsa looks—

Ilsa looks—

Ilsa looks—

Blank. The lights are on, but she's still in the blackout.

Failure to adjust.

I can hear the rain outside, insisting we pay attention. I can smell the liquor on the room's breath.

"What's going on?" I ask.

This brings Ilsa back—but only partly.

It's Parker who responds. "Lights went out, and KK got all freaky with Sesame Street over here."

KK stands up and smooths her French maid outfit. "It was dark. I needed male attention. I was curious if this would be two for the price of one—and, let me tell you, it *was*."

Frederyk looks a little dashed on the rocks by this explanation. Caspian remains impassive.

"I think the window's leaking," Li says.

She points at a juncture where the windowpane isn't quite slipping into the frame. A thin stream of water is running down the wall onto the floor.

"Why didn't anyone tell me?!" I cry, then run into the

kitchen for some paper towels. When I return, I go into full-on sop mode. Li has to step aside for me to do it.

"Do you need help?" Johan offers.

"No! I'm fine!" I say, even as I wonder if the paint is going to have a water stain. Or maybe the whole frame will warp. . . .

"You are *not* fine," Ilsa says. I look back at her and notice she hasn't moved since I walked back in with Johan.

"This isn't a problem," I tell her. I'm plugging the gap between the window and the frame with paper towels. I can get duct tape and seal it properly in a second.

"I'm not saying *that's* a problem," Ilsa replies, pointing at the window. "I'm saying *this* is a problem." She gestures around the room.

"Thanks a lot," Parker says.

"I am not experiencing a problem," KK rebuffs.

Jason releases something halfway between a laugh and a huff.

"What are you saying?" I ask. Because for once, I genuinely don't know.

"I'm saying, why the fuck are we throwing this party? Why are all of these people here? Why do we bother doing all of this, if it's only going to turn to shit? This was supposed to be a recess from the humdrum, but I feel it's just another version of the humdrum. Dress it up however you want—we're still stuck, and I'm tired of it, Sam. I'm tired of you fussing and making nice. I'm tired of KK doing whatever she wants, whenever she wants. I'm tired of trying to figure out if Parker is a red state or a blue state when it comes to my election. I'm tired of Jason taking on the role of inquisitor, when he knows me about as well as Caspian here knows what it's like to have legs or Johan knows how to return your flirtation. For that matter, I'm tired of Frederyk not being what I wanted him to be. He was supposed to shake up your world, Sam—not make a mess of mine."

"Poor Ilsa," Jason mock sobs. I note the bottle in his hand.

"What has Sam's lasagna done to you?" KK asks. "I knew it was trouble."

I leave the paper towels in the gap and walk over to my sister. "Look," I say, "it's been a lot. Do you want to go lie down? We can start dessert without you. . . ."

She swats me away, even though I haven't tried to touch her.

"I don't want to lie down! You're not my parent, Sam—you're my *brother*. This was such a bad idea—I need to go. No, seriously, that's it. I need to go."

I know what she's just stated, but still I find myself saying, "You're leaving?"

"Yes. Sorry."

Then, without stopping to get her keys or her purse or her coat, she walks out of the room, out of the hall, out of the apartment. We all hear the door open and then close behind her.

"I'll go get her," Parker says.

"No," I tell him. "I'll do it."

"Oh, let her have her tantrum," KK advises. "She'll be back. It's not like she has anywhere else to go."

"You're such a good friend!" Jason comments. "You're so lucky to have her! I mean, she's so lucky to have *you.*"

Parker starts to head out. But Li body-blocks him.

"No," she says. "I'll go."

Parker starts to argue, but Li cuts him off.

"I was the only one not mentioned in her roll call of gripes. I've got this. I don't expect you or Sam to understand, but it has to be me."

"What about me?" KK asks.

Li gives her a once-over. "Why don't you stay here and ask yourself that while I go find my friend?"

With that, she leaves us. We all hear the door open and then hear it close.

"Anyone else want a drink?" Jason offers.

Caspian pats the empty space on the love seat, and KK returns to it.

I turn to Parker.

"Don't look at me!" he says. "I didn't do anything!"

I turn to Johan.

He smiles and asks, "Time for dessert?"

eleven

ILSA

"What happened?" Li asks me as I open the door to the roof deck. "Did the lightning suddenly strike you with bitchheart?"

I laugh as we walk through the entryway. I go to the outdoor storage shed, take a thick blanket from it, and then place it over the wet wood bench that sits under the canopy trellis, whose leaves are soaked and dripping. The storm has passed, leaving behind a breathtakingly clear view of the city skyline, and fresh, damp air that does nothing to appease the evil thoughts lurking within my wicked brain.

We sit down on the (mostly) dry blanket. I say, "It was pretty random, actually. My brother came back to the living room, and he gave me that look he has, like nothing's wrong, when in fact *everything* is wrong, and then all of a sudden I hated Sam with a fiery passion. I couldn't stand the sight of his stupid sweet face any longer."

"Does that happen to you a lot with him?"

"No. But when it does, it's fierce." Li always brings the nicest chocolates. I can't do her the dishonor of letting her think I'm better than I am. I admit, "I wasn't suddenly struck with bitchheart. It always lurks within me."

"I don't believe that. Bitchface, maybe. Not bitchheart." She must know that other deadly sin lurking within my heart—greed—because she opens her purse, retrieves the box of chocolates she must have grabbed on her way out, and opens it. I pick the one that I hope is mocha-flavored, and if it's something gross, like one with lemon filling (who would *do* that to the inside of a chocolate?), out of respect for Li Zhang and her uncommon goodness, I'm not going to return it half-eaten to the box.

I take a bite. Mocha! I further admit, "You're wrong. I was born with bitchheart. Sam got all the good DNA."

"Maybe bitchheart isn't so terrible? It will make you a survivor."

"That's what I'm afraid of. I don't want to be a survivor. When the apocalypse finally hits, I want to die first."

"I don't believe that, either," says Li. "When the Atlantic Ocean finally pushes past Brooklyn and takes over Manhattan, the Ilsa I know will be standing on top of the Empire State Building, flirting with sailors and throwing everyone life rafts."

"Doubt it. I'm scared of heights." We're on the nineteenth floor of the Stanwyck, although technically it's the eighteenth floor, since most older Manhattan buildings don't have a thirteenth floor. Those previous generations sure knew how to build superstition directly into the souls of building residents. Eighteen or nineteen—it's still many floors beyond my comfort level. Running toward my fears but never overcoming them: That's how I like it. "I always sit under this trellis because it's in the center of the roof deck. I feel nauseous if I walk near the edge."

"Me too!" says Li. "So what are we doing up here, anyway?"

"I like to come up here because access is forbidden to Czarina's apartment unit. When the Stanwyck went condo years ago, the holdouts who didn't give up their rent-controlled apartments were denied access to the rooftop."

"That's so mean."

"That's real estate. Says Czarina."

"But you have the key to open the door to the rooftop deck. I just saw you use it."

"Czarina had a fling with the landscaper. He had a copy of the key made for her."

"Your grandma seems like a real problem solver."

"What makes you say that?"

"This muumuu. It's so comfortable, I can't stand it. I hope I'm not being vain, but I feel like it looks as good on me as it feels."

"It does. Czarina does wonders with fabrics. She can make any cloth look fashionable and amazing."

"How come she never went into business for herself? She's so talented."

"She did. Years ago. A clothing store with her brother. The business failed. Whatever happened between them was pretty bad. Czarina hasn't talked to her brother since before Sam and I were born."

"Ouch." The silence that follows is Li's acknowledgment of my fear—of what could happen to me and Sam. That we could become like Czarina and the brother whose name she won't even speak aloud. Siblings. Partners. Then dead to each other.

Their falling-out wasn't just over the failed business. It was over who got the rent-controlled Stanwyck apartment that had originally been leased to their grandparents. Czarina won that battle. The price was never seeing or speaking to her brother again.

I say, "Sam and I are nothing alike. I don't know how we're siblings, much less *twins*. I can't believe I ever shared a womb with him. Even in there, he was probably the one banging around the least, giving Mom the least trouble. I retroactively hate him for that, too."

The storm left behind wind. It's chilly up here. The Mary Poppins who is wearing Czarina's purple muumuu pulls a long shawl out of her purse, hands me one end, and we place it across our shoulders so we're almost in a huddle. "Why are you so mad at him, Ilsa?"

"I don't *know*!" I'm not yelling, but I'm close. My skin is cold but my blood is boiling.

I do kind of know.

I'm mad that he invited Parker. He knows how the sight

of Parker hurts me. He knows that Parker moved on, but I didn't. I hate to accept that in the custody battle for Parker's friendship, Sam will always win. I hate that Sam *should* win that custody. I hate that every time I feel like I've moved on from my feelings for Parker, I have some reminder of him from Sam—I see a text on Sam's phone, or hear Sam laughing in another room when they're hanging out and don't think I'm around, or Sam bloody invites him to our last dinner party at Czarina's. It would be so much easier to let go if I didn't have those constant reminders—and brutal for Sam if he was ever forced to choose between us. Nobody wins. I want to blame Sam, even if I know how unreasonable that is.

I'm mad that Czarina and Mom and Dad love us both the same, but they *like* him more.

I'm mad that I always have to share a birthday with him.

I'm mad that Sam got piano lessons and I got dance lessons. He's good enough to get into a world-class music school like Berklee, and I fell flat on my face and gave up. I would never be good enough to pursue my art in a renowned school. Sam *could*—and chooses not to.

I'm mad that we came from the same womb, but he will always get to live with white male privilege with no real consequences if he fucks up, and I will be the bitchheart just for being honest and real with my feelings.

I'm mad that he hurts and keeps it all in. I trust him with my problems. Why can't he trust me with his?

I'm mad for no good reason other than I'm scared and everything's changing, and probably not for the better.

"I think you know," says Li.

"You're right, as always. I'm mad that when anything goes wrong, Sam goes with the flow. I storm out for no good reason, while he stays reliably calm, even when I know for a fact it's not how he really feels. It's insane-making."

"What do you care if he's calm? Isn't that a good quality?"

"Because the calmer he is, the more I look like a bitch."

"Then don't act like one. It's maybe that simple."

"It's *not*. I just feel this anxiety all the time. Acting out is how I express it. At least, according to my therapist."

"There's medication for that, you know. I take it. Helps a lot." She laughs. "Except when there's bad thunderstorms—for me, at least."

Quietly, I say, "I'm scared."

"Of a pill?"

"That it will change me somehow. Filter the world through a duller palette."

"Doesn't feel that way to me. I still have my freak-outs, but overall I feel like I handle the anxiety better since I started medication. It used to cripple me. Now at least I try to deal. The medication doesn't change any situation. It just gives you kind of an extra floor to catch you if you fall." Li softly nudges her arm against mine; she's very comforting. "It's gonna be okay."

I'm still sore, and I still hate Sam's ex-boyfriend. I hate how easy it is for Sam to have a harem of cute boy crushes while I'm still stuck on Parker. Sometimes I'm not even sure if I'm still stuck on Parker or, if I'm being truthful, just stuck on the hurt that Parker dumped me. "Jason Goldstein-Chung said I'm awful. Sam didn't even try to defend me."

"Jason said *KK* is awful. She is."

"Is it horrible that's what I like about her?"

"It's not horrible. It's frustrating."

I let out a little laugh. That was the last explanation I expected. "Why frustrating?" I ask Li.

"Cuz I would like to hang out with you more. KK monopolizes you."

"I don't know about this proposition." I feel a smile coming across my mouth, despite my best efforts to tamp it down. "Could you try to be more awful?"

"Oh hell yes, I could. Let's go back downstairs, and I'm going to, like, crush some Dollys, and put Caspian into a shoe, where he belongs, and straight-up tell Sam, *That lasagna sucked.*"

"You're a beast, Li. I had no idea."

"We should hang out more."

"We *should.* Why do you have to live in Queens?"

"There are trains that go to Queens."

"But . . . so far."

"I've successfully made it from Queens to Manhattan for four years of high school. Trust me, it can be done."

"I hear the Indian food is good where you live."

"It is."

My blood feels less boily. My heart rate has slowed down. I say, "Maybe I don't need anxiety medication. Maybe I just need you around when I need to calm the fuck down."

"Weirdly, helping other people calm down helps *me* calm down. Totally distracts my own anxiety."

"So this wasn't a selfless mission to spaz down the bitch-heart?"

"Not entirely."

"Well, thanks anyway." Thanks for the chocolates and the shawl and the warmth. "It's nice to be up here, in the quiet."

We're looking at each other now, face to face, and we're leaning into each other, and out of nowhere, Li's lips land on mine. It's the sweetest and most unexpected kiss I've ever had. It definitely warms me up. It definitely makes me wonder if there could be more. Her breath smells like she just ate the peppermint-flavored chocolate.

She pulls back. "I'm sorry! Was that . . . okay?"

"It was a surprise. But a nice one."

"Really?"

"Really." I have to figure out my brother before I can figure out Li Zhang and how she's a way hotter mess than I ever realized. I subtly turn my face so she'll know I'm not planning more lip connection—but not so far away that she'll think the future potential isn't there. It is. "Sam doesn't know it, but I'm going to become Maddy Hogue's new nanny and live in Czarina's apartment once the Hogues take possession of it."

"Is that what this is about? That you haven't told him yet? I don't think he'll be mad. He'll be happy for you to get to live here."

"That's the problem. I want him to be mad. I want him to feel. To rage."

"Then have it out with him. Tell him that."

"I don't want us to become like Czarina and her brother."

Li looks me intently in the eyes. She asks, "You know what happens after a seismic event in your life?"

"Everything changes."

"Maybe. But *you* don't. You'll still be the same person you were before it happened, and so will Sam. Your character and heart don't have to change even if circumstances do. It's how you deal with the event that determines whether you can handle the fallout."

That makes both no sense and total sense. "I want to be better than awful," I admit.

Li takes my hand in hers. It's more than a friend's touch, less than a lover's. A tender in-between of possibility. "Let's go face your fears," she says. We stand up. The shawl falls from our shoulders. I never noticed before how silky black her hair is or how sexy her curves are, even under a muumuu. She's checking me out, too. She points at one of the cats on my dress and says, "Caspian's right! Geraldine might really have a lazy eye."

"Is Caspian your favorite at dinner tonight?"

"Of course not. You are."

She holds on to my hand and leads me back inside to the elevator.

When we return to Czarina's apartment, we find the worst-case scenario for Sam and Ilsa's last dinner party.

Sam is playing the piano, accompanied by Johan on a fiddle I think Czarina's third husband (the scamp!) left behind. Parker is crooning into a mic, while Caspian and KK and Freddie are making out on the sofa and Jason hovers in front of Sam, besotted.

This party is a delight.

I was not missed.

So I walk over to the grand piano, and I'm just about to slam the fallboard down onto Sam's prancing fingers, when Li pulls me back.

The music and merrymaking stop. All eyes are on us.

Li says, "Time for the rager we were promised, Sam."

twelve

SAM

I am not against drinking. But I can't say I enjoy it very much when my friends drink excessively.

I'm trying to stay at the piano. Because if I keep playing, no one's going to ask me why I'm not getting plastered. I'm trying to keep it jaunty—some Gershwin, some ragtime.

I don't think anyone's listening.

They are raiding Czarina's liquor cabinet, which, if we're honest, is more of a closet than a cabinet. Ilsa's dispensing its contents to everyone like she's the Florence Nightingale of gale-force nights.

I am not going to be the guy who tells everyone else what they shouldn't be doing. I am sick of being that guy.

I want someone else to be that guy.

I want someone else to step in.

Nobody else is stepping in.

Johan's letting Ilsa mix him a G & T. Jason's swilling whiskey like its post-marathon Gatorade. I am not looking in KK's general direction because I don't want to know what's happening there. Parker has lined up seven beers on the windowsill. Li doesn't seem to be drinking. Neither is Ilsa, but I'm thinking she'll start once everyone else has been given their pillage.

I wish Johan were still playing beside me. That felt good, to be harmonizing without having to open my mouth. His strings. My strings. Vibrations overlapping in the air.

But now he's laughing at something Ilsa's said.

I want to play louder. Drown everything else out.

Impossible.

Maybe that's why I gave this up. Playing with other people around. It wasn't making anything better.

I forgot that.

But that's not really the reason. No, the reason is that audition. That *failed* audition. I'd wanted to go to Juilliard for years. It's the best music school in the city, which to a New Yorker means it's the best music school in the country. My rehearsals were flawless, my preparations impeccable. But as I waited there for my name to be called, I started to drown within the importance of what I was about to do. I got flustered, and when they asked me to come in, I didn't even hear them at first. When I finally *did* hear them, when I finally was given the chance to shine, I sputtered. My thoughts were too loud. I couldn't hear the music. I made mistakes. Probably not that many, but enough to throw me. I was fine—but the audition required me to be great.

When I got home, I couldn't keep it hidden. I told Ilsa everything.

Her response? She told me, "If you can't stand the pressure, then don't put yourself under the pressure."

I think this was her way of being supportive. But it also kicked away the last of the beams that were holding me up.

"Can I make a request?"

It's Jason at my shoulder. Jason, whose breath is proof enough of how far gone he is.

"Sure," I say.

"How about 'How Can You Mend a Broken Heart?'"

I shake my head. "I don't know that one."

"'Guess I'll Hang My Tears Out to Dry'?"

I'm sensing a theme. I say, "Jason. Stop."

He slaps his hand down on the side of the piano. "Fuck it," he says. "I'll settle for 'You Belong to Me'—either the standard or the Taylor Swift version."

"I think the Taylor Swift song is 'You Belong *with* Me'—"

"Well, fuck YOU."

I'm playing "Smoke Gets in Your Eyes," and I keep playing "Smoke Gets in Your Eyes."

"Jason, I think you're drunk," I observe.

"Well, I think you're sober. *So there.*"

"Is there a problem here?" Johan sidles over and asks.

"No problem," I say.

"There wasn't until you came over," Jason spits out.

"What does that mean?" Johan asks.

"I think it's pretty straightforward," Jason replies. "It means *you're* the problem. Jesus. You can't just come over here and take him. You have to put in some time."

"Nobody's taking me anywhere," I point out. The song is too fast under my fingers. I hit a wrong note. I keep going.

Johan moves to get the Maker's Mark bottle out of Jason's hand.

"Here," Johan says. "Let me take this and bring you some coffee instead."

But Jason won't relent. He stabs out with the bottle. "*She* sent you over here, didn't she? I HATE YOU, ILSA!"

"Feeling's mutual!" Ilsa calls out.

Jason lets go of the bottle. It knocks the G & T out of Johan's hand. There's a shattering on contact, then another, more muffled break when the bottle and glass hit the floor.

"Shit!" I yell. I stop playing and jump off the piano bench. "What else can go wrong?"

Before I can get an answer, I go to the kitchen for more paper towels, a broom, and a dustpan. I notice that it isn't two seconds after I stop playing that the stereo starts to blast a cake's worth of Drake. Li's been waiting by the controls, waiting for her opening.

When I get back, Johan and Jason are shoving each other, working the glass and the drinks further into the floor. There aren't enough Altoids in the world to cover up the smell of intoxication coming from the rug.

"Stop it!" I shout, wondering why no one else is halting

them. I mean, this mess is universally recognizable as *not good*. And Ilsa's mixing Li a drink.

Johan stops, but Jason's still in his space.

Parker takes the broom, paper towels, and dustpan from my hands.

"You take care of Jason, I'll take care of the spill," he says.

It's worse than a spill, I want to tell him. We're never going to clean this up. Never.

It's a stain.

We're leaving a stain.

But if I don't get Jason out of here, he's going to leave even more of a mark with the Maker's. So I tug his sleeve, pull him away from Johan.

"*What?*" Jason yells.

"I'm giving you a time-out," I tell him. "Come with me."

He stumbles under my grasp. KK laughs, but I can't tell whether it's at Jason or because Caspian is tickling her with his lower jaw.

"Where are we going?" Jason asks.

"My room," I answer. There's too much to drink in the kitchen.

"Oooooh. I remember *your room.*"

I am sure that what he remembers is not the same as what I remember. That's what made it so hard to break up with him. He is remembering sex and kisses and being together. What he can't possibly remember is how lonely I still felt. Even when he was there, I kept thinking, *This isn't enough.* Because it didn't stop me from worrying. It didn't block the intricately

115

self-directed fears from my mind. Sometimes he could distract me . . . but I always knew it was a distraction. As soon as he left—sometimes before he left—my mind would return to its magnetic north, pointing toward all the things that could and would go wrong.

"I've never seen you drink this much," I say as I steady him through the hallway. "Is this a new thing?"

"Just getting ready for college!" he replies.

There are echoes, deliberate or not, of what I told him when I called off our relationship. I dwelled on the fact that he was going to Boston in the fall and I was staying, as a way of not getting into the fact that we were in different places already. It didn't seem fair to tell him that I didn't think he really knew me, because I was the one who'd kept my thoughts to myself. I hadn't let him in, so I couldn't blame him for not understanding what was inside. I blamed it on Boston instead.

When he gets into my room, he goes straight for the bookshelf. "Yup," he says, then takes a collection of Nathan Englander short stories off the shelf. "I gave you this, you know."

I nod.

"Remember the night I got it for you?"

I don't. But I tell him I do.

He thumbs through the book for a second, as if our own history is written inside. Then he puts it back on the shelf and looks at me hard.

"Why did you invite me here?" he asks.

"Honestly, to prevent more damage to the living room. No ulterior motive, just interior motive."

He shakes his head. "I don't mean *here*. I mean tonight. What got me back on the guest list?"

"I wanted to see you."

"*URRRRRR*," Jason groans, making a buzzer noise. "Try again."

Try again?

"Because . . . it's been too long. And we're leaving soon, so—"

"*URRRRRR*. Not it."

"What—you don't think it's been too long?"

"*URRRRRR*."

"What?"

"*URRRRRR*."

I am getting more and more annoyed. "What do you want me to say?" I ask.

"I want you to tell me why you invited me."

"I already told you! It's because I wanted to see you."

"*URRRRRR*."

"Because you're my friend."

"*URRRRRR*."

"Stop it!"

"*URRRRRR*."

"Because I wanted you here."

"*URRRRRR*. Be honest."

"I am!"

"*URRRRRR*. One more time: WHY DID YOU INVITE ME?" he shouts.

"Because I felt bad!" I shout back. "Okay? I FELT BAD."

"DING DING DING!"

"But I also wanted to see you!"

"No, no—don't cover it up now. You *felt bad*. And do you think having me here should make you feel *less* bad? Is that fair? Shouldn't I, as the brokenhearted party, be the one who gets to determine how you feel?"

"You're *not* the brokenhearted party."

"You dumped me!"

"It wasn't working!"

"It was! I was just up against too much."

Now it's my turn to groan. "That means *it wasn't working!*"

"No. It means that your sister was against me and you wouldn't go against her enough for me to win."

Yes, Ilsa thinks Jason is boring. Yes, Ilsa always believed he was the safe choice. Certainly, Ilsa was still trying to sell me on other boys while I was dating Jason. She actively encouraged me to break up with him, leaving morning Post-it notes on the bathroom mirror that said *Today's the Day You Get a Better Boyfriend!*

But Ilsa was not the reason I broke up with him.

"It's not that," I tell Jason now. "It was never that."

Jason laughs. "It was *always* that. Whether you see it or not. Your blind spot is five-foot-six tall, without heels."

"I can think for myself, okay?"

He comes over to me, starts to give me a hug. I don't fight it, but I don't really encourage it, either. This is our relationship in one action: He thinks he's helping, and I think it's awkward.

"Untether yourself," he whispers in my ear.

Like—

Like—

Like it's that easy.

Like he has any idea what he's talking about.

Like he didn't want me to be tethered to him instead.

Like I'm not already tethered to everyone.

Only that's not actually how I see it. It's not like there's this cord that connects me to him, or to Ilsa, or to anyone else. No. When I picture it, it's more like I'm one of those old illustrations of Gulliver, tied to the ground with hundreds of different ropes. Ilsa controls some of them, sure. But others are manned by the friends I care about. Some are staked by *strangers* I care about, or are tied to the fact that every time I check the news it feels like the world's going wrong. Tie after tie after tie. And I just lie there on the ground, giving them more time to get more ropes. I rarely struggle. Because the few times I tried to cut the ropes, I ended up cutting myself instead. Which was not what I wanted, either.

Jason doesn't know any of this. Ilsa would, if she'd only open her eyes. Parker has moments when I think he understands, and other moments when he seems too deep in his own life to be considering mine.

Jason hugs me tighter.

"I miss you," he says. "I miss this."

It takes a good minute before he realizes I'm not hugging him back. And even then, he disengages without acknowledging it, acting like we've both let go at the same time.

good you'll have to keep hurting them again and again until they become numb to it, indifferent to it. I didn't invite Jason over here tonight to hurt him. I thought this conversation had been completed months ago. But now I see we're going to have some form of it for many years to come.

"Give me one reason we can't try," he says.

And because I want to end this smaller conversation even if I can't end the bigger one, I say, "Because I like Johan. Because I am trying things out with him."

This does not go over well. Jason guffaws, stumbles back.

"Johan? Do you realize you're going after #Stantastic's sloppy seconds?"

"I didn't know they'd been together until tonight."

"Oh, wow. Then you have no idea who you're dealing with, do you? Do you have any idea what he did to Stan?"

"I'm sure I would have read about it."

"You *did* read about it, Sam! Don't you get it? Johan is #TheDictator!"

I look at him blankly.

"With a *k*," he clarifies. "#TheDicktator."

"Am I supposed to know what you're talking about?"

"Jesus, Sam! #Stantastic's only been griping about #TheDicktator for months. #ThePassiveAggressiveOlympics? #TheDevilAteAllMyPringles? #Couldn'tBreakHisHeart BecauseHeNeverHadOne? Haven't you been following *any* of this?

I shake my head.

"That was Johan. #TheDicktator was Johan. He's, like, a

He goes on. "How well do you know him, really?" Then he comes back closer. "I know you much, much more."

"*URRRRRR!*" I shout, crossing my arms in front of me. And once I do it once, I can't stop. "*URRRRRR! URRRRRR! URRRRRRRRRRRRRRRRRRRRRR!*"

It's a shockingly effective way to repel an ex-boyfriend. He stumbles back, looks a little green. Then he recovers his footing. But his expression . . . still a little green.

"Oh shit," he says. Then, without another word, he bolts to the bathroom.

"The toilet, not the sink!" I yell out. Then I follow at his heels, in time to see him make it to the porcelain throne. He retches. And retches. Then pukes his guts out.

"Oh, Jason," I say gently, kneeling beside him. He doesn't have any hair to hold back, so I stay there and hand him a wet washcloth when he's done.

"I don't feel too good," he moans.

I pat him on the back. Flush. Get him a towel. Let him slump against me.

"He's evil," he mutters.

"Yeah, I'm sure this is all Johan's fault. He has a voodoo doll of you and is sticking a needle down its throat right now."

"He's a dicktator!"

"Understood."

"I couldn't leave without one more party here," Jason says.

"I know, I know," I tell him. "Because this is the last one. This is it. It's over."

It feels strange to say it. And even as I'm saying it, I'm still not sure what it really means.

"It's hard to think of you without it." Jason slumps against the bathroom wall. "It's hard to imagine you without this fortress."

"It's not a fortress. It's an apartment."

"But the two of you made it a fortress. And neither of you have any plans to leave."

I start to protest, but Jason waves me quiet.

"No, no," he goes on, "let me speak. You two have always been impen . . . inpend . . ."

"Impenetrable?"

"Exactly! We all know you should be going to Berklee, right?"

Not this again. "No," I say. "Just because you're going to Tufts and you wanted us to stay together, it doesn't mean I had to go to school in Boston."

"You are SUCH a fuckface, Sam! Will you listen to me? I'm not talking about you and me being together. I'm talking about it being a great fucking school. A great fucking *music* school. And when it came time to go there, you choked. No. That's wrong. You didn't choke. You fucking *strangled yourself*. Because you didn't want to leave your fortress. It's what the two of you have most in common: You can't find the way out, even when it's right there in front of you."

Jason has never talked to me this way. *No one* has ever talked to me this way.

"Fuck!" he moans, then leans over the toilet again. He retches a couple of times, but nothing comes out.

"False alarm," he says as he slumps back against the wall.

His eyelids are drooping. "Look," he says, "I'm not talking anymore about you and me being together. I still believe that we should be together, but that's not what I'm talking about. I'm talking about you getting out. You need to get out. Because if you don't get out now, you never will. Even your drunk ex-boyfriend can see that."

"Well, I'm not going anywhere right now," I say. His collar's gotten messed up, and I fix it.

He smiles. "Appreciated." Then he closes his eyes.

"Hey, friend," I say. "Maybe the bathroom's not the best place for a nap?"

"Right right right."

I help him up and get him to the bed in my room. He collapses as quickly as a Macy's balloon filled with sand.

I think he's out as soon as he hits the pillow. But as I turn off the light and start to tiptoe away, he says one more thing.

"It was really great to hear you play again," he tells me. "It's so stupid you stopped playing for other people."

I thank him. And I allow myself to say that, yes, it was.

thirteen

ILSA

Typical.

Sam's always had a secret Spidey sense alerting him when I'm on the warpath, allowing him to dodge my mad mood like the adorable, handsome coward he is. It's too bad my twin wasn't another girl. Our menstrual synchrony would put us on the same PMS-bitch-rage schedule and then we could quickly and efficiently have at it like siblings should. Tussle, scream, fight, pull hair, get it out, then done and besties again, until the next time.

This duck-and-run maneuver of Sam's is getting old.

I'm ready to pounce. He sensed it, and escaped to the bedroom with Jason.

Jason Fucking Goldstein-Chung.

I'm insulted.

And anyone thinking I am being too hard on Jason should know this about him:

1. He's cheap. One time he took Sam on a "surprise date" to Fire Island, but Sam had to buy his own train ticket, and while Jason did buy their lunch, that lunch was stale sandwiches from the train station because Jason couldn't spring for a nice restaurant at the lovely ocean where he'd dragged my brother. Jason's not poor, either. He's had his own website design company since he was twelve. Hashtag, AnnoyingOverachiever.
2. He smells weird. Because of the cheap cologne he wears to ward off the smell of his insecurity.
3. He's rude to old people. I don't care if Jason's rude to me, but being rude to our parents and Czarina is unforgivable. Only I am allowed to do that, and only because I know to profusely apologize afterward. What kind of boyfriend shows up for a family dinner—wreaking of *Insécurité pour Homme,* I might add—and proceeds to tell the grandmother how she could decorate her apartment better, and then proclaims himself a math genius by explaining to his boyfriend's parents that they're really not making enough money to send their kids to college, and they should think about taking on extra jobs? A smelly one, that's what kind.
4. He knows every line of every song from *Xanadu,* the musical.
5. I take back #4. That's maybe the one decent quality of Jason's.

My boobs feel heavy and my stomach crampy. PMS is definitely contributing to my hostility—but that doesn't mean the hostility's not deserved anyway.

"Throw me a brew," I call to Parker. He tosses me an unopened beer bottle. I pop it open and take a good long chug, finally ready to be a part of my own party.

Everybody is tipsy and having a good time. What Sam's cooking couldn't accomplish, reliable ol' alcohol has. Johan fiddles the tune of Prince's "She's Always in My Hair" while Parker croons the lyrics, shooting his sexiest smile my way. KK and Freddie are slow dancing, with Caspian snuggled into the crook of KK's neck. Li is in her happy place: She's pulled out the knitting bag she always carries and continues work on a stunning teal sweater sleeve.

Parker sings, *"Whenever my hopes and dreams / Are aimed in the wrong direction,"* and I don't know why it took two years to finally hit me, but at last, I hear it. He's so off-key!

Parker wiggles his index finger at me, an invitation to join him in the song.

"Don't do it, Ilsa!" KK calls over to me. "Do *not* fall into his Prince-croon trap. Again."

It was Parker singing "Purple Rain" during Sam's and my birthday karaoke party our sophomore year that undid me, and caused me to undo every button holding up my clothing later that night.

I shrug at Parker's invitation—*nah*—and take another sip of beer. "'Kay, KK," I say.

If I want to be better than awful, I should start with Parker.

Stop resenting him and wanting him and feeling hurt by him as much as I've wanted to be back with him. Let it go, Ilsa. (#6: Jason's love for *Frozen* sing-alongs. Honestly. Do that in private like everyone else, in the shower, where it belongs.) (Also, *Elsa* with an *I*—Ilsa: superior spelling.)

The song ends. "Want to break into the empty studio apartment across the hall?" I ask the group. They cheer, except for KK, who would never allow herself such common enthusiasm. Enough alcohol, and sneaking into a small unit with a crap view can sound appealing. Again, except to KK.

"I'm bored," whines KK.

Caspian rubs himself against her cheekbone. "Don't say that," he whispers.

"You're not bored," I tell her. "You're in the best threesome of your life tonight."

To the rest of the group, I say, "Shall we?"

Li, Parker, Johan, KK, Freddie, and Caspian come to the door. "Bring the fiddle," I tell Johan. "In case you're inspired."

We go into the hallway. Parker asks, "We're going to Mr. Bergman's apartment, right?"

"Yes," I say.

"Did he finally move?" Parker asks. Mr. Bergman was a "confirmed bachelor" who'd lived at the Stanwyck longer than Czarina.

"If by 'move,' you mean to Mount Hebron Cemetery in Flushing, Queens, then yes," I say. "Mr. Bergman moved."

Parker does the sign of the cross over his chest. "Rest in peace, Mr. Bergman. He was a good dude. Used to give me and Sam the free movie passes his family sent him every year at Hanukkah. Said he hated 'the picture show' and why didn't his family give him opera tickets instead."

And now I'm mad at Sam for something else. He got grumpy Mr. Bergman's free movie passes.

I walk to the front door opposite Czarina's apartment, and there is no real crime happening here. I simply turn the knob, and the door opens. The building workers only finished clearing out Mr. Bergman's apartment this morning. I knew they wouldn't remember to lock the door. I knew they'd want the quiet, secret refuge for themselves until the real estate agents swoop in and Mr. Bergman's apartment goes up for sale.

We step inside. I flick on the light switch, but there's no bulb in the ceiling fixture. Through the light coming from the hallway, Parker spots a small lamp on the floor. He turns it on. I close the door behind us.

The best part of Sam and Ilsa's dinner party will be when Sam returns to the living room and finds I've stolen his guests away. The good guests, not Jason Goldstein-Chung. Whenever Sam finally emerges, he'll see we can have a great time without him, just like he showed me.

I remember trying to peek into this apartment as a kid. I'd be standing at Czarina's front door waiting for her to let us in, and Mr. Bergman would come outside to go to the elevator. From those brief flashes, I remember the apartment seeming bigger than it does now, in the dim light and with no furnishings. "Depressing view," says Li, standing at the windows with an air-shaft view of another wing of the Stanwyck building.

It's no wonder the guy was not very friendly (except to cute boys).

"He probably didn't see much sunlight for the last fifty years," says Parker, mind-reading me as always.

"We're afraid to live 'cause we're afraid of dyin'," says Johan.

"That's deep," says Parker.

"That's Dolly," says Johan.

"I want to see the kitchen," says Li. She steps inside the alcove kitchen, attached to the main room.

"I want to see if Mr. Bergman left any beers in the fridge," says Parker, following Li.

KK says, "I didn't know it was possible for an apartment to be this small. It's smaller than my bedroom. I feel like I'm suffocating."

"Let's go back to Czarina's," says Caspian.

KK bolts out the front door, with Freddie/Caspian in tow. "Air! I need air!"

I turn to Johan. We're alone at last. "I want to know your intentions toward my brother," I say.

"Lascivious," says Johan. The guy just keeps making me like him more and more, dropping words like *lascivious*. Johan could practically be a third member of Flight of the Conchords, he's so way-below-the-equator odd, and cool, and confused-charmed by the native New Yorkers.

I point to the corners of my lips, like they're sore, and I emit a deep cough, hoping Johan will get my meaning: cold sore. "Then . . . have a talk with Sam first. Because . . . you know. He'll dodge you because the subject makes him uncomfortable, but if you bring it up first, he'll be fine to tell you. Be safe."

Johan's so naturally pale and it's so dark in the room, I don't know if I've embarrassed him with my comment, but he's definitely made the connection, from the awkward shifting in his legs. He whispers, "I tried to kiss him earlier, but he backed away at the last second. That must be why."

Is it? Okay, sure!

My work here is done.

I'm hardly mad at my brother at all anymore. Just needed to let it go with some old-fashioned sibling payback. Fake STD story, real FTW for Ilsa.

Parker and Li return from the alcove. Parker's holding a can of Ensure. "No beer," he says.

"But lots of protein drinks!" says Li.

Johan picks up his fiddle. "I was told you two were once competitive ballroom dancers," he says to me and Parker.

"Once upon a time," I say.

"We could still be champions," says Parker. "Later tonight, right, Ilsa?"

"Show us what you've got," says Johan.

"Perfect dance floor," says Li, gesturing to the parquet flooring below our feet, unobstructed by furniture.

Johan starts to play. A tango.

Parker holds out his arms for me to step into position. I hesitate. I don't want to be sucked back in.

Whoa! Seeing Parker resume that familiar position after all this time, I realize: I don't have to be sucked back in for anything more than a dance.

Sam has always been the boy-crazy one in our twinship. He never lacks for male admirers, and his life sometimes seems like a constant revolution of flirty messages and cute boys wanting to know him better. It's never been that way for me. Most boys are scared of me. Parker wasn't. In turn, I was boy crazy for only Parker. Literally, crazy.

Finally, I get it. I can dance and be friends with Parker again because I'm over him. I feel love for him, but not *in* love.

"I don't want to go to any dance-off with you later tonight," I confess to Parker before I can step into his arms.

"I've been sensing that. So let's dance it out now, then," says Parker. "One last time."

I place my hand in his and feel his arm around my waist. It feels good, and right. Because it never needs to be more again.

We dance.

fourteen

SAM

I realize I should leave a wastepaper basket by Jason's head, so I duck back into the room and put it in place. He's already snoring in a post-drunk oblivion.

I head back to the hall and am surprised by how quiet it is. I'm even more surprised to find the living room and the kitchen empty.

The party, it appears, has left me.

And what I feel is—

Actually—

Relief.

Ilsa has probably led them to the roof. Most of our parties end up on the roof at some point.

I could follow them.

I could.

But I guess I don't want to.

Instead, I clean up. First I tend to the stain—it looks like

Parker tried to mop it all up, but even if he stopped the bour-bonic plague from spreading, it didn't whisk all the Maker's away. I find some rug cleaner and do the best I can. Then I gather the bottles, gather the plates, gather the glasses still waiting for the next sip. I turn my mind off this way—if I focus on the dishes, I don't have to think about anything else. I am in control of this. I can make things better by straighten-ing up. That's all I have to do.

The walls aren't that thick. I can hear life going on, but at a remove.

I'm tired.

All the caps are back on the bottles. All the bottles are back in the cabinet. I check the ice bucket—the ice is only half there. I empty it into the sink. I turn on the hot water, to make the remains of the cubes melt faster.

I don't know what I'm doing.

I guess I'm staying inside the fortress.

Jason's words are annoying me, and not because they're off base.

I wish Johan had stayed behind to keep me company, but I'm not surprised that he didn't. I wish Parker would pop down to check up on me, but I'm not surprised that he hasn't. I wish Ilsa had left a note, or some indication of where she was tak-ing the party. Maybe she figured I'd guess. Or maybe the lack of a note is a message in itself.

I'm sure I could find them, but I don't try.

I hear music from across the hall. I think Mr. Bergman must be having a party. Then I remember—there's no way Mr. Bergman is having a party. And I don't think rowdy wakes are a Jewish thing. Which means either his relatives aren't very observant or Ilsa has commandeered the apartment. A place of her own.

Fine, I think. Let her have it. Let her have all our guests. Let the party officially be hers.

Because maybe I'm done.

I've been rinsing off plates without thinking. I've been loading the dishwasher without thinking. I've been leaving the platters out to dry, knowing that I'll be the one to dry them. It's Ilsa's job to dry, but I'll do it.

My hands are busy, but really the thing I'm holding the most is that phrase: *I'm done*. It's breakable. I don't know exactly how to grasp it. I don't know what to do with it. But it's mine.

I brew a new pot of coffee. I put some petit fours on a tray.

There was always supposed to be one more course for this, our recess from the humdrum. One last course. One last hurrah. Because you always want the guests to leave on a sweet note. Because you always want to make them a little more awake, so they can get home.

I could go home, too. This apartment is not, technically, my home. But if I'm being honest with myself (and why not be honest with myself?), that other room has only *technically* been my home. This apartment is where my life has happened. The retreat that became the destination.

I look around the kitchen. I have been so happy here. I have been so sad here.

I guess that's what home is.

And I—

I—

I feel like I'm leaving it.

Which is different from knowing we're moving out. That feels like the apartment leaving me. This life, leaving me.

But now—

Now it's me who's thinking about doing the leaving.

I have never looked for a way out. All these years, all the sad times—I always felt that it had to be something inside of me that was off, something inside of me that couldn't appreciate the life I had. Ilsa would taunt me for playing it safe, for being the good kid, for doing the right thing. But, honestly? None of the other options felt present. None of the escape routes. I could see the doors, sure. But I was sure they were locked. And because I was sure they were locked, I never tried the knobs.

I see the error in this logic now.

I've always had a good life. But maybe it's not *entirely* a good life if I constantly feel like one wrong move, one wrong choice can destroy it. A good life should be able to withstand more than that.

But—

But—

But what am I saying?

What am I telling myself?

I go back out into the living room. I straighten the pillows on the couch. I refold a blanket KK knocked over to sit down on the chair. Things are almost back to the way they were.

The easy thing would be to smash bottles, to break lamps.

To yell FUCK IT to the world and create some damage. But I've tried that. I've tried breaking things to feel better—and found that it only feels better while things are breaking, not the next moment, when they're broken. It's a release that leads to nowhere. It's not the answer.

Neither is taking it out on my own body. I learned that, too.

But maybe a clean room isn't the answer, either.

The music across the hall gets louder. There's talking, but I can't hear the words. I could just collapse on the couch. I could head back to my non-room at my parents' house. On the surface level, I'm exhausted. Spent. But there's also a tug inside urging me to see this through. To find the way out, whatever it is.

I tell myself: I'm tired . . . but I still have things I need to do.

I tell myself: I'm sad . . . but I still have things I need to do.

I look around the apartment—everything is in order. I put fresh napkins and forks out on the dining room table. I make sure the sugar bowl and the artificial sweeteners are represented. I make sure the coffee has brewed. I move it onto a cart that Czarina has designated to be used for the coffee service.

It's all set. And then I think of one more thing. One more touch. Another factor for the grand finale.

Delicately, I take Czarina's champagne flutes from the glass shelf on which they usually perch. Each flute is as thin as paper and as clear as air. I cannot hold one without feeling nervous—and that's precisely why I am taking them down now.

If there's no way to stop being nervous, I have to learn to be okay with being nervous.

I'm still careful—each flute gets its own passage. When I'm done, they make it look like a chandelier has been spread across the table.

It feels right, and I take some satisfaction from that.

Part of me wants to leave it like this. Without anyone else around, symmetry can be achieved. Under these conditions, nervousness can dissipate. It can be just me and my well-dressed table. Me and my—

Me inside my—

Fortress.

No, I tell myself.

Look for the door.

Find it unlocked.

I step across the hall, and enter Mr. Bergman's apartment. In the dim light, I can see Parker and Ilsa tangled in a tango. Li is knitting, but her eyes are decidedly on the dance. KK is going through Mr. Bergman's drawers. Frederyk and Caspian are thumbing through a book of Fran Lebowitz essays that Mr. Bergman left behind. Johan is the only one who turns to me when I come in. He smiles, shifts in his seat. Making room.

"There's coffee and petit fours and champagne for a toast," I announce. "If anyone is interested, please return to our table. The corks will be popped in five minutes."

I turn around and leave before I can get any response. I head straight back to Czarina's, and her kitchen.

For about a minute, the music goes on next door, but then it stops. I hear them all come back. Most head straight to the dining room. I try not to worry about the champagne flutes as they take their seats.

"Do you need any help?" Parker pops his head in and asks.

"I need so much help," I answer, smiling.

He comes all the way in.

"Sorry we absconded," he says. "I was going to get you, but figured you and Jason might be stuck somewhere in the past. How'd it go?"

"The past has been relinquished. The future is being reached for."

Parker raises an eyebrow. "That so?"

I nod.

"You up to something?"

"Yes, but I'm not entirely sure what it is yet," I tell him. "How about you? You and Ilsa dance partners again?"

He laughs. "I think we're good to tango, but not sure I'd say we're gonna be partners again. To quote a late great, I wanna dance with somebody who loves me. And I have a sense that I'm not her baby tonight. Which is as it should be, I think. Best-case scenario is that it's less of a mess than it was before—and that's what you were going for, right?"

"I guess?"

Parker offers me a level glance. "Look, when it all comes down to it, I think you took the breakup worse than I did.

140

Maybe worse than Ilsa did. I don't know. I'm not saying it was the cause of you being so low, but it definitely happened during your blue period. And because me and your sister were so busy hating each other, I think that—I guess what I'm trying to say is that maybe she and I could have helped you more if we'd teamed up for it. She and I apart didn't help you at all. And I know we never talk about it, and I'm not saying we have to talk about it right now—but being back here and all, it makes me think about that."

"My blue period," I say. I've never heard anyone refer to it like this before. It's not something we ever talk about.

"Yeah."

I can't get off of it. I need to know more. I ask, "What do you know about my blue period?"

Parker's proceeding with caution, but still, he's proceeding. "I think both Ilsa and I know more than you think we know, Sam. But we never knew how to bring it up. We knew you hurt yourself, but . . . we were taking your lead when it came to talking about it. We thought if you were keeping something a secret, it wasn't our right to force it out of you. At first, I figured you were talking to her about it, and I'd guess she thought you were talking to me about it. Since we weren't talking to each other, it wasn't like we could compare notes. Although now I wish we'd gotten over our bullshit to at least check in. We kinda fell down on the job, didn't we?"

It's like suddenly I have to rewrite the past year of my life. I thought Czarina was the only person who knew. She was the one who took me to get help. She was the one who lied and said we'd gone on a spontaneous jaunt to London—with some spontaneous Manhattan "shopping trips" away from the apartment after that.

I genuinely thought everyone had believed that.

Especially Ilsa.

A chant springs up from the dining room: "CHAM-PAGNE! CHAM-PAGNE! CHAM-PAGNE!"

"I need to get out of here," I tell my best friend, who doesn't really know me as much as I should have let him.

"If you need to bolt, I can bring in the bottles," he volunteers.

I shake my head. "No, not right this moment. But soon. I need to find somewhere else to be. To live."

There's that smile again. "Well, that's easy," he says. "Come to California with me."

"Yeah, I'm sure Stanford allows people to apply in June."

"CHAM-PAGNE! CHAM-PAGNE!" (I think Ilsa's voice is loudest of all. Or maybe that's KK's.)

"COMING!" Parker hollers.

I go to the refrigerator and take out two bottles of champagne—Czarina always has four waiting for impromptu celebrations and/or consolations. I know she'll notice them missing. I'll just have to explain. I think she'll understand.

"I'm serious about California," Parker says, grabbing the bottles so I can push the coffee cart.

"I know you are," I say. That's all I'll commit to.

We head into the dining room. Parker lets me go first, so

he can have my back. As soon as we get there, KK yells, "Finally!"

I disregard her—something I've trained myself to do over years of practice. Instead, I look at Ilsa. She seems a little bit curious and a little bit confused—she knows champagne was never part of this party's plan.

"Coffee, anyone?" I ask.

"Do you have decaf?" Caspian inquires.

"Decaf makes no sense!" Ilsa and I answer at the same time.

"They never have decaf," Parker adds.

"Champagne first," KK decrees.

"It's not your party," I tell her.

"Come on, brother," Ilsa chimes in. "First, toast. Then, caffeine and sweets."

"CHAM-PAGNE! CHAM-PAGNE!" Caspian starts to chant again. No one else joins him, and the sock looks down, dejected.

I check out the faces at the table. I think they all want champagne.

I decide to be a gracious host.

"Champagne it is, then," I say. "Who wants to do the honors?"

It can't be me, because I am always startled by the pop. It can't be Ilsa, because she sucks at opening anything involving a cork.

"I can," Johan volunteers.

I watch as he effortlessly opens the first bottle and pours

champagne into each of our glasses. I like him even more when he spills a little when he gets to KK, and looks momentarily horrified.

Watching him, part of me thinks, *Aw, c'mon, Sam. Stay.*

But then I hear Czarina, of all people, counter this, and tell me it's not worth staying in place for someone else. I've seen it with her—I think she would have been off in Paris years ago, if it weren't for me—for *us.* When she told me she was going to move there—"a secret, just between us," she said—she didn't have to point out that she'd been waiting for me and Ilsa to head off to college. I knew. In the same way she must have known that I appreciated it, even if I didn't say anything, and even if I wasn't planning on leaving the city for college.

She wouldn't push me out of the nest. But she *would* take the nest away. And if I ended up building another nest nearby, so be it.

But—

Well, I'm not sure I want to build that nest anymore.

Because I'm not sure I *should* anymore.

"Are you going to make a toast?" Ilsa asks. She gestures to everyone's glasses, ready to be raised.

"Yes," I say, taking a deep breath. Not avoiding the nervous—plunging right into it. I lift my glass, and everyone else echoes the movement.

"Here's to leaving!" I say.

"To leaving!" most everyone else calls out.

But not Ilsa.

What are you doing? the look in her eyes asks me.

She doesn't understand.

Even though most everyone is already drinking, I raise my glass again to clarify.

"And not just to leaving this apartment—to leaving New York. To leaving the fortress. To exiting the comfort zone and finding the world."

I drink up. Parker moves to clap at that, forgetting he has a champagne flute in his hand. Johan looks curious. KK looks doubtful. Frederyk looks blank, but Caspian looks encouraging, as does Li.

Ilsa still hasn't taken a sip.

"What are you talking about?" she asks, putting her glass down.

"Maybe I'll go to California," I say.

KK pipes up. "What do you mean, *California*? Like it's all the same. Northern California and Southern California are two different things. If you're not going to L.A., that's like saying you're moving to New York when you're really moving to Rochester."

"When did you decide this?" Ilsa asks.

"Two minutes ago?" I answer.

Be happy for me, I want to tell her. *Just let me do this.*

"So this is, like, an impulse. It's not actually a *plan*," she says.

"I think it sounds like a great idea!" Johan proclaims. And I'm ridiculous, because while I appreciate his support, I also don't want him to be quite so enthusiastic about me moving away from the city in which he lives.

"I like Northern California more than Southern California," Caspian volunteers.

"Me too," Li says.

"Well, of course you do—you're *New Yorkers*," KK groans, with no shortage of exasperation.

"And you're not?" Parker asks her.

"I'm just biding my time here," KK replies.

"Nobody's going to California," Ilsa insists.

"Actually, I definitely am," Parker points out.

"You *don't count*."

Parker raises his hands in surrender. "Noted. But, hey, this isn't about me."

Ilsa decides to shoot even though his hands are up. "You sure you didn't have anything to do with this? You sure you're not the cause of this delusion?"

"Whoa!" Parker says. "Way to be supportive of your brother."

"My brother isn't going anywhere! We all know that."

"I don't know that," Johan says.

"Me neither," Caspian adds.

"You two don't know anything," Ilsa says.

"Way to tell them, bitch." KK applauds.

"Ilsa—" Li starts.

"How about me?" I interrupt. "Don't I know?"

"Fine," Ilsa says. Then she raises her glass. "But first I think it's my turn to make a toast."

fifteen

ILSA

I want to give a toast, but I'm afraid.

Sam took out Czarina's collection of nineteenth-century Baccarat champagne flutes. The ones she keeps on the highest shelf so they may be seen through the cabinet window but never touched (except on Czarina's birthday and the leap days), the gold-rimmed crystal goblets of great historical family importance. They were brought to America by Czarina's great-grandmother and her sister, who hid them under their skirts while escaping some early twentieth-century Eastern European pogrom. The glasses are Czarina's most prized possession.

The legend of the libation chalices is a lie, of course. It's not actually possible to hide *eight* crystal champagne glasses tucked into two skirt linings *and* climb a mountain pass to freedom without breaking the glasses *or* dying from the stress and exhaustion of trying to keep the glasses silent to soldiers' ears.

I'm sure my ancestors had amazing skill. I'm just saying there are holes in the story. And that Czarina watched *The Sound of Music* too many times after inheriting the flutes from her own grandmother. Fact and fiction have always been blurry for Czarina, which is one of the many qualities I appreciate about her.

Her notorious temper, however—I'm terrified as hell of that. I don't mind being on the receiving end of her lower-scale expressions of irritation, like when she finds out her booze supply has been depleted or her precious Persian carpet has a new, dark booze stain. I can even deal with her medium-scale fury when she learns that Sam broke out her best champagne, the authentic and very pricey French kind that Czarina doles out on her birthdays ending in 0 or 5, and on occasional New Year's Days for her New Year's Eve "hair of the dog" hangover cure. But I cannot, and will not, be on the receiving end of Czarina's nuclear tantrum if any of the drunks at this dinner party table breaks one of her precious champagne flutes.

I've had eighteen years of taking the blame whenever Sam and/or my hijinks caused trouble, but this infraction—should it happen—I absolutely will not be responsible for. If something happens to one of these glasses, it's on Sam.

Who bloody thinks he's moving to California!

Holding the sacred goblet intimidates me so much that my hand shakes as I raise it in toast. But the loose grip puts it in mortal danger, so I tighten my hand and say, "To Sam's wishful destination, the Sunshine State!" I'm too busy worrying about the flute; I have no idea how to finish off this toast.

Before I can continue, Caspian says, "If you mean California, that's the Golden State."

Little bitch.

"The Golden State!" I continue. "Land of drought, traffic, smog—"

"Those are more SoCal problems," KK interrupts. "I think Sam sees himself farther north." She laughs. "You'll hate it there, Sam," she says to him. "It's so not you."

Sam says, "Coming from you, KK, I'll take that as Northern California's most ringing endorsement yet."

Li says, "I don't know why the Bay Area is referred to as Northern California. It's more in the middle. If you look at a map."

Johan says, "That's true! I've gone hiking up in the Siskiyous. True Northern California is a whole other world from the Bay Area. May as well be another country."

Parker begins to sing, *"I left my heart in San Fran—"*

"Can I finish, please?" I ask. So much rudeness. Everyone's glasses are still raised to toast. Let a toaster finish her damn toast already.

The interrupters around the table hush. Shit, with their raised glasses and expectant expressions turned in my direction, it's like they think I am going to say something profound. (Those are the toasts *by* Sam, not *for* him!) I say, "To Sam! Who hates too many sunny days—"

"Again, that's Southern California you're thinking of," says KK. I might kill her.

"It never rains in Southern California," Parker sings.

"Let Ilsa finish her toast already," says Li. "My arm hurts."

"And I'm thirsty for champers," says Caspian.

I take a breath and try again. "To Sam, who can't survive ten whole days off the island of Manhattan—"

This time it's Sam interrupting me. "That was seven years ago, and I broke my leg! I couldn't stay at Camp Ticonderoga!"

He totally could have. He left me there, alone, for five additional days of mosquito bites, basketmaking, and pre-adolescent lesbian crushes on camp counselors.

I ignore him. "To Sam, with dreams of California, but who breaks out in hives if he's outside a twenty-block radius of Lincoln Center."

"Cheers?" says Li, and takes a drink.

"Cheers," the others add on, except for Sam. They all take a drink. Sam's eyes narrow at me, and then he takes a drink. As do I.

"Quality champers!" exclaims Caspian.

"Really? You tasted it?" asks Li, eyeing Freddie.

KK licks her lips. "Ah, much better than that cheap Trader Joe's crap that Ilsa swipes from her parents' fridge."

"Those are wine coolers our parents keep in the fridge," Sam tells KK.

KK says, "I drank wine coolers with Ilsa?" I nod at her. KK gasps. She glares at Sam. "You could have allowed me my ignorance."

"And spared my joy at your horror?" Sam asks. "I think not."

The champagne is indeed delicious, but I can't relax enough to enjoy it. Neither can Sam, apparently. He puts his glass down and asks me, "So what makes you think I can't survive California?"

I say, "I guess you could if a precise plan was set out for you. But just going there on a whim? No way. Not only would you never survive . . . you'd never go. So no big deal, right?"

"It *is* a big deal," says Sam.

"I'm not stopping you from this fantasy," I tell my brother. "Go, if it's that important to you."

"Where I go isn't the big deal," says Sam. "It's that you know me so little you think I can't get there."

"*Whoomp, there it is,*" sings Parker.

No one knows Sam better than me. What's he PMSing about?

"Of course you can get there," I say. "There's planes, trains, cars, whatever. I'm not talking about transportation."

"Neither am I," says Sam. "I'm saying you have me nestled so comfortingly in your *idea* of who I am, you have no idea who I *actually* am. I might be capable of moving to California for no good reason other than it's not here and I have no idea what I'd find there."

"This California idea is very reverse *Felicity*," says Johan.

"Who?" everyone else at the table says.

Johan says, "Do you Americans not even know your own pop culture? *Felicity* was a TV show about a girl from Palo

Alto, California, who had a crush on a guy from her high school. So she followed him to New York for college."

"Stalker-y," says KK. "I like it."

Johan says, "That show was one of the reasons I wanted to go to college in New York."

"To stalk a guy?" Parker asks.

"To stalk an experience completely foreign to anything I'd known before!" exults Johan, who is very red-faced from all his alcohol consumption. He places his index finger and thumb together like he's holding a maestro's baton, and calls out, "And for the music! The nightlife! The danger!"

"The pizza!" says Caspian.

"Don't talk about carbs or no more noogie noogie for you," KK says, not seeming to understand that the double use of words like *noogie* nixes sarcastic intent.

"Speaking of carbs, where's those cookies your little friend brought over earlier?" asks Li. I retrieve the tin of Junk in da Trunk cookies, place it in the middle of the table, open it, take one for myself, and hand the tin to Li. She takes out a cookie and has a bite. "These are, like, the definition of disgusting. And possibly the best cookie I've ever had."

She passes the tin to Parker, who takes one and has a bite. "I'll pay for this later. For now, hurts so good."

He passes the tin to Sam, who passes it on to Johan. "I'm trying *not* to go into a diabetic coma tonight," says Sam.

Johan has no such qualms. He takes a bite of a cookie. "Is that *potato chips* I taste in here?"

I say, "Yeah, and chocolate chips and butterscotch morsels and malted milk balls and peanuts and pretz—"

"Stop," says Johan. "Allow me the illusion my teeth aren't going to fall out after I finish this cookie."

"I wish Jason wasn't passed out in Sam's room," I say. "Cuz these cookies would certainly be the end of him."

"JUST STOP!"

There's a moment of silence after Sam's outburst. Sweet Sam never behaves so rudely.

"Stop what?" I ask him.

"Stop being mean about Jason. Stop interfering."

"Interfering?" I ask, taken aback. "You do what you do with Jason no matter what I say."

"So maybe don't say anything? Maybe keep your opinions to yourself and let me live my life? If a guy I like is a jerk, let me find out on my own. I don't need your help, Ilsa."

Of course he needs my help. I'm eight minutes older. I think I know a little bit more about the world than naïve Sam.

"Fine," I say.

Not fine.

Even more than the pain I feel that Sam apparently thinks I don't get him is the betrayal I felt that Sam never trusted me enough to tell me he was hurting so badly. His silence made me feel like a failure as a sister. And I was a failure, because I never had the courage to just ask him if he wanted my help. Czarina probably didn't ask him, either—she just went ahead and helped. Sam and Czarina have always been the Dynamic Duo, not Sam and his twin. Sam and I have no twin telepathy, no twin identical moves. We're just people who came from the same womb and were raised in the same apartment(s). He got the better room—in our grandmother's apartment, and in her heart.

"Someone's been secretly harboring some resentment," Dr. Caspian informs us.

"What's *your* secret?" Johan asks Caspian. I think he's trying to take the attention off Sam, who looks frustrated. "You know what I'd like to know, Casp? When you and your conquests go at it"—here Johan eyes KK—"how do you, you know, complete the transaction? Do you have a special—"

"Handler?" Parker asks, using finger quotes.

Everyone laughs except for Freddie and Caspian, whose stitched mouth is not capable of such an expression. Freddie's look, however, falls somewhere between murderous and mutinous. But KK saves his pride. "Believe me, Casp 'n' Freddie have *all* their parts in order." She looks to me. I know that look. It's KK's *I need to throw someone under the bus* expression. "You know who has secrets, Sam? Ilsa. Ask her where she'll be living when you think you'll be in some part of California you have yet to determine because you don't understand the state *at all*."

Sam says, "You mean Ilsa's intention to become Maddy's nanny and move into my room when the Hogues take over this apartment?"

"You *knew*?" I say. And finally, after all these years, he acknowledges what the family knows but never says aloud.

Czarina's spare room is essentially Sam's room. The favorite's, and no one else's.

Sam says, "Of course I knew! I was just waiting for you to tell me. Typically reckless Ilsa, thinking she can rock the boat with secrecy and then offer a grand reveal that will send everyone spinning."

"You becoming a nanny is absurd . . . ," says Li. "Why would you squander your time in a job you probably don't even want, if you really thought about it, in a place you already know?"

"What else should I do?" I ask her.

Parker offers, "Go to college. Wander the world. But don't stay here for no reason other than you wanting Sam's room for your own finally."

It's so much more than that.

Is it?

Why am I doing it?

KK says, "I'm with the rest of these dummies on this one. Don't be a fuckup because that's what's expected of you, Ilsa."

"But that's the very definition of reckless," says Sam. "And that's our Ilsa."

"SHUT UP!" This time the outburst comes from me. "Being a nanny is hardly a reckless job."

Li says, "Agreed. But there's also no point to it, for you, at this stage of your life."

Johan says, "And you're probably taking the job from someone who really needs it."

I feel ganged up on. Quietly, Li says, "Don't give up on yourself so easily."

"I don't know what else to do," I confess.

I meant about myself, but Li is thinking about the bigger world. Li says, "These are scary times. Do something. Rise up. Protest. Participate. Believe in something bigger than the silly goings-on of rich people at the Stanwyck."

"Hey!" says KK. "I'm one of those people."

"Exactly," says Li. "Who are you going to be, Ilsa?"

"Maybe you should go to California with Parker and Sam," Johan suggests.

"No," Parker and Sam both say.

"But hey," Parker adds, looking at me. "I have you to thank for my five-thousand-dollar scholarship toward expenses at Stanford."

"How so?" I ask.

"Our best dance?" he says.

"The merengue," I say.

"That's the one. You know how college financial-aid guidebooks always mention obscure scholarships no one's heard of because it's hard to believe they exist?"

"I guess?" I say. I never cracked a single guidebook for college. I left all the problem-solving aspects of my potential college future to my parents.

Not okay, Ilsa.

Parker says, "There's a Merengue Society of New York City that sponsors an annual scholarship. They picked me."

"Based on what?" I ask. "An essay about the merengue?"

Parker says, "Yes, I did write an essay about the merengue."

I was kidding about that.

"No shame! But the deciding factor was the video I submitted from our competition days. So, my parents also say thanks. For shining me so bright you saved them five K a year."

"That's amazing, Parker. You deserve it." I mean it.

The breakup still hurts, but much less so. Sam was so embarrassed and caught between a rock and a hard place right after. He blamed me, of course. I'm the reckless bitch who always gets blamed. Sam doesn't need to know about the part of the breakup that Parker and I kept to ourselves.

It started when I was a week late. I told Parker. He was supportive, as always. He went to the pharmacy and brought over a test for me to take. I peed on the stick. But during the few minutes we were supposed to wait for the result, I freaked out. I asked Parker if we could go ice-skating in Central Park. We did. It was winter, and snowy, and magical, and I wanted to stay snuggled in Parker's arms forever.

When we got back to my bedroom and looked at the result, it was positive. It was strange. I felt relief rather than panic. My worst fear was confirmed, but somehow I felt like it wasn't the worst thing that ever happened to me. Maybe it was the best. It would give me a future. I'd never want to trap Parker, or keep him from going to college and achieving his dreams. But I knew that no matter what happened in our lives, I'd always have this piece of him.

For a black guy, Parker certainly turned pale that afternoon. "It's your choice," he said. But I knew which choice he wanted.

We sat on the secret for three days. I didn't want to make an announcement until I knew for sure. We went to Planned Parenthood. We wanted to show how responsible we were by going there before talking to our families.

This time, the test came out negative. The doctor explained I'd probably had a false positive on the store-bought test. I was supposed to read the test results within the time frame specified on the box. We went ice-skating instead. The doctor said that it wasn't unusual for evaporation lines to appear on the test strip as the urine dried. That people who read the results after the recommended time had elapsed often confused the appearance of urine evaporation lines with a faintly positive test line.

Parker broke up with me a week later. He wasn't ready to be in a relationship that serious. I wasn't, either—but I would have done it anyway.

Sam raises his glass. "A toast to Parker and his merengue scholarship!" he says.

The group raises their glasses to Parker and downs another sip. Except for KK, who abstains from the declaration of "Cheers" but double-downs the champagne.

And then, Sam lifts his empty glass.

I see his signature—

—hesitation.

I—

Er, universe, what should I do—

But—

—I am scared and frustrated and confused.

Sam takes aim—

—and smashes Czarina's precious handblown crystal heirloom champagne flute against the wall.

sixteen

SAM

Because I am tired of her seeing me as the favorite. Because I am tired of both of them—Czarina *and* Ilsa—seeing me as the favorite. Because this is goodbye, because this is *done*. Because I'm so tired of worshipping breakable things. Because I wanted to see the impulse through. Because I wanted to see the look on all their faces. Because I wanted to do something that I've kept inside of me so they could see what's been inside me all this time. Because it's not like Czarina is going to take them to Paris, anyway. Because Czarina told me not to tell Ilsa about Paris and because I actually followed her orders. Because I'm not sure whether I want to go to California or whether I just want everyone to be able to believe that I'll go to California. Because it's almost festive to throw the glass against the wall when you're done with the drink, like there's no going back from the toast you've raised. Because I am tired of Ilsa looking at me like I'm an emotional invalid. Because I am twisted enough to think that if I become the one who doesn't care, then she'll become the one who cares, that we exist to achieve balance as a pair because we are so deeply imbalanced as individuals. Because I know that's not how it works. Because why bother smuggling something around the globe and across the decades if you're only going to keep it under glass? Because I think it'll make Parker laugh. Because I might as well scare off Johan now instead of later. Because when Ilsa says she's happy for me, she never sounds like she means it.

The moment after it happens, I should be terrified. The moment after it happens, I should feel remorse. I should run to pick up the pieces.

But instead, now that I have everyone's attention, I decide to pose a question.

"How do you leave?" I ask. "How do you get out of the fortress?"

Ilsa is still looking at me in shock, so I know she's not going to start. It's Johan who takes the first shot.

"As you know," he says, "this is something I have some experience in. And I'm not saying there's a right way or a wrong way to do it. But if you're asking how I did it . . . well, let me see.

"I always had the destination in mind—the question was, how would I pay for the ticket? I don't mean that literally—although I guess it's there literally, too. But I mean it more like, what's the thing that's going to get you from where you're

161

stuck to where you want to be? And don't get me wrong—when I say *stuck*, I don't mean that my parents were mean or my friends were lame. I loved them all. But I loved the idea of setting off, the idea of New York even more. And I realized my ticket was music. Even when I was twelve, thirteen, I knew it was my ticket. Not that I loved it more than my family or my friends—but I knew that of all the things I loved in my life, it was the one that could travel with me."

I remember feeling that way about music. I loved losing myself to it—but then I guess I felt that was a dodge, that I wasn't supposed to lose myself. Which I'm realizing was as unfair to me as it was to the music.

Johan continues. "I also told myself that leaving doesn't mean what it used to mean. I'm half a world away from my home, right? But I can still call them every day and see them every day, if I want. And that's the key part: if I want. I get to control it. I haven't left entirely, just by leaving." Johan stops. "I know I'm not answering your question. How do you leave? You tell yourself you can go home whenever you need to. You tell yourself you're trying something out. And you find something you love to take with you. You give yourself a chance to be someone else, but you don't turn against the person you were. You give yourself room to breathe, and then you breathe. Did I have to go all the way from Cape Town to New York City to find that? Probably not. This is just one of the many ways it could have worked. But it *has* worked. I followed my dream. And here I am. So you need to follow your dream."

"I love that," Li says. "*Follow your dream*. It's such a great way to trick yourself!"

"What do you mean?" Johan asks, before I get a chance to.

"Well, think about it. We always talk about our dreams as if they come from somewhere else. *Follow what you think*—no, that's too straightforward. We don't trust ourselves enough to do *that*. But *follow your dream*—there's a beautiful lack of acknowledgment in there that, guess what, *dreams are ours*. They're not being beamed to us from some cosmic cable station—they're coming entirely from our minds. Saying you're following your dream is just a way of giving yourself permission to follow your mind. And I'm all for that. Here—let me give you an example."

She turns to Ilsa. "When I say that I've dreamed about you, Ilsa, what I'm really saying is that I want us to be together in a way that's even greater than what we've been before. When I tell myself that following my dream led me to kiss you, what I'm really saying is there's always been a part of me wanting to kiss you, and I finally let it take control. Opportunities are the openings that appear without our control, but what we do with those opportunities—that's up to us." She turns back to me. "So how do you leave? You let yourself leave. It's as simple as that."

She goes back to looking at Ilsa. So do I. *They were kissing?* Part of me wants to cheer. And part of me, honestly, wants to tell her to stop stepping on my territory.

"I'm not sure *simple* is the right word," Caspian says. "Maybe change is simple for some people, but not for everyone."

"Did you just call yourself a *person?*" KK asks. "That's priceless."

Caspian ignores her and leaves his button eyes on me.

"You must find your allies, because sometimes leaving is . . . hard. People believe you are a certain thing, and if you're not who they want you to be, they can get confused, like my mother, or they can get angry, like my father. It's hard for me to explain to you where I come from. It's not an apartment like this."

"Is it more like a drawer?" KK can't help herself.

"JUST SHUT YOUR UGLY MOUTH!" Caspian screams at her. Then he turns to the rest of us. "I apologize. It was a mistake to engage with her, on all levels. What I mean is that our home is much more . . . modest. My father is a janitor. My mother works at a dollar store. Their expectation was that I would work, so I have worked. Contributed. But when I understood my . . . situation, they were not understanding. My father mocked me. I don't mean once or twice. I mean for years. But leaving wasn't an option, because in order to leave, you need money, and at age twelve, I didn't have any money. Even now, I don't have much.

"But my mother—she became my ally. I started off in secret, and then she became a part of the secret. Because that is what allies do—they allow you to let them in on the secret, and then they become a part of the secret until you start to feel that maybe it doesn't need to be as much of a secret anymore. More than anything else, that was the fortress I was in. I think you understand."

I nod.

"You are not alone, Sam. There are some people who are very alone. I was very alone until I understood how to be un-alone. You already have allies. With some, it may take time for them to understand. Some"—and here he looks at KK—"are probably not worth the time. Get rid of those people who doubt you. Then go forward."

"I doubt you," KK says. "Does that mean you're getting rid of me?"

Caspian nods. "Absolutely."

KK sighs. "Kicked to the curb by a sock! I guess that's what it's come to." She glares at Ilsa. "There—I tried something different. Happy? Never again."

"You really can't pin this one on me," Ilsa replies flatly.

"Why not? But I digress—your widdle bwother asked a question, and it would be rude for me not to answer."

I try to tell her she doesn't need to bother, but she shushes me.

"Oh no! This is all so very interesting. Do you know what I learned? I learned that leaving is bullshit. Because you always take yourself wherever you go."

"What a revelatory thought!" Parker interrupts. "I think you might be the first person to ever discover that."

"All I'm saying, Sam, is that the problem isn't *here*—the problem is *you*. Say what you want—I have everything I need in this city. I don't need to go anywhere."

"Because you have money," Parker points out.

"Yes, because I have money."

"What about the rest of us?" Parker asks.

"Well, I'd suggest you get more money."

"That's not helpful," Parker says.

"Actually, I think it is," Li puts in. "It just goes to show why you need to leave your fortress every so often. Otherwise you can be tricked into thinking it's the whole world."

"What?" KK asks with mock innocence. *It isn't?*

"Build a wall!" Parker says. "That's the way to do it! Build a wall around your comfort zone so you never have to leave it! Build a wall between yourself and the things that scare you the most, the things you don't want to look at. Oh, and while you're at it, build a wall to hide the things that scare you the most about yourself—that way, you'll never have to look at them! Build a wall to keep your friends trapped with you, even though—I have a little secret for you, KK—they always find a way to leave, don't they?"

KK doesn't launch a counterattack. She doesn't laugh at him. She doesn't say anything. She's silent, trying to stare him down, then looking to Ilsa for support that Ilsa doesn't give.

Parker turns to me. "This is your chance," he says. "You've never had a chance before to make your own way, not like this, not a completely blank slate. Just go for it. What you did to that glass—it can't be undone. But heading off somewhere when you're eighteen—that's not necessarily permanent. You're not choosing a path, just a few steps. And you go from there. We're all improvising to some degree. But you have to leave the house to find a path."

I wish he hadn't mentioned the glass, because now I am feeling sorry about the glass.

I turn to Ilsa. "How about you? What are your thoughts on the matter?"

I'm asking her thoughts because I can tell there are plenty of them going on in her head at the moment. I can tell she's quiet not because she's disengaged, but because she's fully engaged. I want to know what those thoughts are. Because I want her to find an escape route, too. Not the same escape route—I know that. But any escape route.

"You want me to tell you how to leave?" she asks.

"Yeah."

She shakes her head. "What do I know about leaving, Sam? The only times I've left, I've been with you."

My instinct is to say, *That's not true.* But when I think about it . . . is it possible that it's true? Except for that separation at camp—is it possible that every time we've left the fortress, we've done it with each other? I've had a solo trip or two—but Czarina's never been one to give Ilsa a solo trip just because I got one. (Especially not if one of the "trips" was to get help.) Even the excursions *within* New York have felt like joint excursions. Like the time we went down to this club to see Rufus Wainwright sing from the Arthur Russell songbook (my choice), and when I went to the unisex bathroom, I found written on the stall, *Sam, if this is what it's like to go south of Houston, let's just stay uptown and order in.* Or the time she wanted to go to Queens to see some Christmas decorations and I decided it would be better to have a Bring Your

167

Own Light dinner party, and create our own display. Because Queens was far, and it was cold out.

When Maddy let slip that Ilsa was going to be her new live-in nanny, at first I was jealous—not that I wanted to spend any more time with Maddy, but that Ilsa had found an angle that would allow her to stay. But the more I thought about it, the more depressing it felt. I wanted to call Ilsa on it, to tell her she was sacrificing her future to cling to her past. Then I imagined her lobbing the same accusation my way . . . and I couldn't think of an effective way to deny it. It would have been one thing to stay in Manhattan to study music. But to stay in Manhattan because I couldn't think of anywhere else to be . . . that, I see now, is not a great plan.

I really wanted this party to be our last hurrah, for it to make me ready to pack up and go. I guess, without admitting it to myself, I invited Jason to help me say goodbye to the past, Parker to help my sister say goodbye to the past, and Johan to help me see what could be up with the future. Only . . . it's not as simple as that. Caspian's right, in a way—things can only be as simple as the emotions we bring to them.

"We're on the cusp," I tell Ilsa. "Don't you want there to be something different on the other side?" Then I worry I've made it sound like we both have an appointment with the afterlife, so I clarify, "I love this apartment—truly, madly, deeply. We made it into something spectacular, which is not something many people get to do. Czarina let us do that. Throw dinner parties. Pretend we're in this world. But I don't think staying here's going to be the answer. Do you?"

seventeen

ILSA

"Where should we go?" I ask.

My brother and I will have no choice but to skip town since he's gone and broken one of Czarina's sacred flutes. Who's the reckless twin now? She'll blame me, of course, but make up for it on the back end by resenting Sam and me equally, perhaps into eternity. When she grabs on to one, Czarina will hold a grudge for a very long time. She hasn't spoken to her own brother since before Sam and I were born. Some might call that stubborn. I call it dedicated.

"We shouldn't go together," says Sam, and I immediately snap, "I *know*." I wasn't saying we should go anywhere together, and truthfully, after tonight, I'm ready to be far away from my brother for a good long time. For both our sakes.

Except on our birthday in January. We've had eighteen birthdays together so far, and on our eleventh, we made a pact to always be together to celebrate the day. Our parents made us sign the pact—it can be seen framed and hanging on their kitchen wall—because it was the rare day Sam and I weren't squabbling as hard as we were playing together. Give a kid that much cake and of course they're going to commit to a lifetime of birthdays with their sibling, regardless of the future reality of the promise. I admit I want the birthday streak to go on for as many years as possible, even though I accept the unlikelihood that Sam and I will annually be found at the Central Park boathouse doing a January polar bear run around the water wearing only shorts, T-shirts, and sneakers.

"Except for our birthday," says Sam, and I immediately love him again. "Shall we consult the hat, Ilsa?"

"The hat! Of course!" I jump up from my chair and retrieve the long pointy black hat from the coat closet in the foyer while Sam retrieves some index cards and pens from the kitchen. We return to the table at the same time, with Sam having also retrieved another bottle of bubbly.

"That had better not be a wine cooler," warns KK.

"Czarina doesn't even know what a wine cooler is," says Sam. "But as penance for her beloved glass that I willfully broke, I downgraded us to the C-list champagne bottle from her fridge." He hiccups a little, good and tipsy. "California Brut."

Parker, whose parents are wine enthusiasts, gasps. "Czarina stocks domestic champagne in her fridge?"

Sam says, "Yes, but only for guests like her lawyer or the Stanwyck's condo board." He looks at me. "Do you want to explain the hat, or shall I?"

KK groans. "I'll do it, you bores. One year for Halloween,

170

Sam went as Harry Potter and Ilsa was the Sorting Hat. They kept the hat, and the family uses it at parties to play Where in the World, a really fucked-up *Dora the Explorer* game of hollow adventures, where no one actually goes anywhere, but they talk for a long time about where they could go, all because of the magic hat's suggestions."

"Your enthusiasm is delightful, KK," says Sam. "Now, would you like to explain how the game works? Or if it's so boring to you, I bet Jason would love a nap cuddle buddy back in my room."

KK convulses momentarily at that last suggestion, as do I. Then she says, "I'm staying. If only to hear about the jail where the twins will be going once Czarina sees what you've done to her glass. *Sam.*" Dear, loyal KK. There's no reason to adore her, other than that I do. If I don't, I fear no one else will. She passes the index cards around the table, along with a pen for each person. "It works like this. Everybody write down the name of a place on a green index card, and a thing you might take there on a pink index card."

Johan says, "This feels like Mad Libs. But for fate."

"Pastel-colored fate," says Parker, looking at the pink and green index cards.

"Pastry fate!" says Li. "My parents don't want to hear it because they want me to be a doctor, but I'd like to be a baker. Not now, but maybe in the future. Can we also write down a profession?"

"Great idea," says Sam. "But no. The idea is to discover what you'd want to do based on the place and the thing, and not have it suggested to you."

Li frowns slightly.

"But I think you'd make an excellent baker, Li." I go on, "The place should be real, somewhere you could find on a map."

Sam says, "That means, no Boulevard of Broken Dreams, no Galaxy Far, Far Away, no Salome's armpit. *KK*."

I say, "And the thing can be anything except—"

Caspian says, "If you have to qualify it, then it can't be *any*thing."

I would smack that little bitch if I thought it would actually wound him.

I continue, "Any*thing* that's not an electronic device like a phone or computer."

"What about my Fitbit?" asks Li.

"What about it?" Sam asks.

"Can I take it?"

"To count your steps going nowhere?" asks KK. "Take it. The Fitbit: the muumuu's perfect accessory. Someone tell *Project Runway*."

I suggest, "Wear that Fitbit proudly but don't write it as a choice for the magic hat. We want less technology-oriented options."

"Aha!" says Johan, scribbling on his paper. "I've got a good one."

I write down my choices—Paris, and feral cat. (Because I feel like Geraldine with the lazy eye, on my dress, has suggested it.)

"This gel pen writes like a dream," says Li. "My hand is practically having an orgasm."

Sam says, "Czarina is a pen collector. That's one of her

favorites, from an office supply store in Tokyo that she loves. She always comes back with dozens of different styles of pens."

"Dammit!" says Li. "I was just writing Tokyo as my place. Now I have to choose someplace else."

She could have kept Tokyo as her place, but now that she's announced it, she obviously can't. Li crosses out the word she'd just written, then uses her spare hand to shield the replacement place she's writing on her index card.

I don't know if it's because everyone's drunk enough or because they're just nice and used to Caspian by now, but no one goes for any obvious comments when Freddie has to write Caspian's choices, since his sock's hands don't possess the dexterity to do so themselves. But we see Freddie eyeing us, challenging us to make a cheap joke.

Once everyone has written their choices, I go around the table holding the hat, for the index cards to be dropped into. "Who wants to go first?"

Caspian raises himself into the air. I step to him. Freddie's free hand dips into the hat.

"Choose one green card and one pink card. If it's one of yours, put it back in the hat."

Caspian groans after reading his cards. "I assure you, neither of these choices is my own."

"What'd ya get, Casp?" KK asks him.

"North Korea and pastrami sandwich. What am I supposed to do with *that*?"

"Introduce New York deli to the oppressed," says Li. "Humanitarian work, obviously."

"Puppetarian?" suggests Johan.

"Proletarian?" suggests Parker.

"Shut up," says Caspian. "I don't want to go to North Korea."

"The sock-puppet passport challenges alone—" Parker says.

"SILENCE!" says Caspian, making a shushing gesture.

"He doesn't like to be called 'sock puppet,'" says KK.

"SILENCE!" says Caspian again, this time giving KK the shush.

"Don't self-hate," Johan advises Caspian. "Embrace your identity."

"Grip it like a tube sock," says KK.

This game was not intended to cause meltdowns. So I move to the next person, to get Caspian out of the line of fire. "Let's get out of North Korea. Much as those needy people could use the pastrami sandwiches. And, Caspian, I think you'd look divine handing them out." I offer the hat to KK, who draws a pink card and a green card.

"Ooh, Miami!" she calls out.

"Look closer," says Sam, who somehow knows how to put a KK-attracting scent on the exact card he wants her to choose.

KK looks at a bottom corner of the card, where another word is written. "Miami . . . OHIO?" She tosses her card in Sam's direction. "I don't think that's even a real place." She looks at her other card. "And I don't think a metronome's a real thing, either."

"It is," says Johan. "Look closer at that one, too."

KK looks closer. "Wind-up metronome? Come on, you're making this shit up. What's it, like a transit card you need to get to wind turbines?"

Johan and Sam laugh. Sam says, "It's an instrument that musicians use to keep time."

KK says, "Keep it *where?*"

Parker says, "In the Top-Secret Time-Travel Lab at Miami University of Ohio."

"Time travel!" says KK. "Now we're talking. Let's ask the Sorting Hat *when* to go somewhere, not *where* to go."

"Where would you go?" Li asks her.

Without missing a beat, KK says, "Salem witch trials. Whenever ago they happened."

There's a pause around the table as we digest this choice. Finally, *"Why?"* I ask.

"I love those little white hats they had to wear," says KK. "With the bows under the chin? Super practical and fucking adorable."

There's nothing to do but move on to the next person. I stand before Johan, who dips into the hat and retrieves his cards.

"Nova Scotia. And feral cat."

"Geraldine!" Caspian hisses. "I know that was your sugges-tion." Add psychic to Caspian's gifts.

Johan says, "I'm not sure where Nova Scotia is, to be hon-est. Is it fictional?"

Li says, "Only in the sense that the Anne of Green Gables series took place there." She sing-songs, "Best books *ever!*"

Sam asks Johan, "Are you trying to pass for American?"

"Never!" Johan exclaims.

"Ignorance of Canada is usually reserved for its neighbors to the south," Parker tells Johan.

"So Nova Scotia's in Canada?" Johan asks.

"Yes," everyone else says.

Johan says, "Well, I'd be delighted to have a feral cat there with me. It could be my muse. I'll write melodies for it to bounce around to, and I'll let it nap in my fiddle case for maximum cute appeal for listeners wanting to hear my melodies and drop a few dollars' donation into the case."

"It feels like you'd be cheating on Dolly if you let the cat hang out in your fiddle case," says Caspian.

Johan says, "I assure you that Dolly would only celebrate me letting a feral cat reside in the case dedicated to her music."

"My turn," says Parker.

I go to him and he retrieves his cards.

"Bhutan . . . and a Slanket? What's a Slanket?"

Li says, "They're the best! They're long blankets that are also, like, pajamas that fit over your whole body and you can zip into. Very cozy."

"Where's Bhutan?" Caspian asks.

"Near India?" Parker asks, looking to Li to affirm his answer and not because she's Asian but because she's the smartest person in the room.

But Li shrugs. "Never heard of the place."

It's KK who informs us. "Yes, it's near India, in the high Himalayas, bordering Nepal and Tibet. It's a Buddhist kingdom filled with monasteries, fortresses, and stunning mountains and valleys. Bring the Slanket as a gift. They're very poor but the nicest people in the world and appreciate any Western luxuries. Fill your coat pockets with pencils to give away, too—easiest way to get a radiant smile from a kid."

There's another pause around the room as we digest this unexpected compassion from KK. "You've been to Bhutan?" Sam asks her.

"Yes," says KK. "I told my parents to tell people I was in rehab, but really I was on a spiritual quest. And getting killer calf strength from all the mountain climbing."

"Sometimes I think there's hope for you," Sam tells KK.

"Fuck you," she tells him.

Sam dips into the magic hat. "I think I'll go to . . . Prague! With a . . . bowling ball? I love that. Wandering around the city in search of a bowling alley in Prague, and finding a bowling partner—"

"Let Caspian be your bowling partner," says KK. "He'll crush it."

"Or be crushed by it," adds Johan.

"That's the hope," says KK.

"The monstrosity to my right is no longer a sentient being to me," says Caspian about KK.

"The monstrosity to my left should remember he's a fucking sock puppet who can't actually feel, much less perceive, sentience."

"More champagne," says Parker, holding up his glass. "Soon enough, none of us will be able to feel anything, either."

Sam refills his glass as I step over to Li, who pulls out her cards. "San Juan Bautista, California, and a unicycle. Where's San Juan Bautista?"

Sam says, "Central California. *KK.* It was a mission town where one of the crucial scenes in the Hitchcock movie *Vertigo* took place."

"More important," says Parker, "it's also a quick distance from Gilroy, California, the garlic capital of the world, and the sweetest-smelling place you'd ever want to visit."

"Better than Hershey, Pennsylvania?" Johan asks.

"Better!" says Parker. "It smells like every pasta dish you've ever loved."

"STOP TALKING ABOUT CARBS!" yells KK. Everyone ignores her.

"I'd ride the unicycle from San Juan Bautista to Gilroy!" says Li, pleased. "And have burned off all the calories for all the spaghetti with hella tons of garlic I'm going to eat when I get there. Oh, I love this game."

I love her for loving my favorite game.

I'm the only person left. I sit back down at my seat and take out the two remaining cards. "Andalusia, and yarn." I feel confident that the first card was what Parker wrote down, and the second was what Li wrote down. What is the magic hat trying to tell me?

"Andalusia's not a real place," says KK. "Someone made that name up. Sounds like a fairy world."

"Andalusia's a real place," says Parker. "It's on the southern tip of Spain, opposite Morocco. It's where flamenco dancing originated." He looks at me, and gives me that smile that melts me. "Ilsa's best dance."

I was never a great competitive ballroom dancer, but when I was at my best, it was because I was dancing the flamenco. The sultry, powerful dance where the female is the star. Sam says, "It's not a bad idea, Ilsa. Go to Spain for a while and study the art you love the most!"

Li says, "Or come to Taiwan with me next month. To study knitting."

Taiwan! What the? Someone believes in me enough to think I could learn to knit?

Johan asks, "Taiwan is known for its knitting schools?"

Li says, "No, but my great-grandma's house is. She's a boss knitter. I go to hers for a few weeks every summer. You should come with me, Ilsa. See something else of the world beyond Manhattan. Go to a place that's completely foreign to you. Learn to knit some scarves."

Manhattan is such a huge universe unto itself, I've never given serious thought to traveling or living anywhere else. That's not true. I've given serious thought to it—but never formulated any realistic initiatives to make that wish come true. I mean, I applied to schools that would take me elsewhere. But I had no actual intention of going. Maybe that's what's been most reckless about me all along. Not that I'm flighty, but too rooted. It's Sam I've accused of playing it too safe. Maybe I should have been looking more closely at myself.

"I couldn't afford that airfare," I say. I have babysitting money saved, but not *that* much.

"I bet Mom and Dad or Czarina have frequent-flyer miles they'd give you," says Sam. "Although, if you and Li are going

179

to be anything more than friends, impulsively going away to visit her family might not be the smartest way to find out."

When have I ever taken the smart approach?

Are Li Zhang and I more than friends?

Our lips touched, but just for a second.

It felt like a second that changed everything I knew and understood about myself.

It's not like suddenly I'm a lesbian.

But suddenly I'm not as straight as I assumed I was.

Suddenly I'm more open-minded than when I started the evening.

Just as suddenly, we hear some keys being tapped on the piano. Sloppy keys. Our heads turn and we see Jason slumped at Sam's piano. He looks up and says the one thing he knows for a fact that only I am allowed to say to Sam. Jason says, "Play it, Sam."

eighteen

SAM

The song that Jason's playing (badly) tells us that, as time goes by, the fundamental things apply. For evidence of this, we're given a kiss and a sigh. I've always been clear on the kiss, a love-story standard. But the sigh has always confounded me. Is it a sigh of pleasure or a sigh of disappointment? Which is the more fundamental?

I stand up to relieve the keys from Jason's fingers but am stopped when Johan stands up as well and asks me to dance.

Everyone is watching. For that reason, I can't say yes. And also for that reason, I can't say no.

So instead, I don't say anything at all. I let him walk me over the glass shards I created by hand (in combination with the wall). I let him hold me like it's our last night in Casablanca, and the whole nightclub is watching to see what we'll do. At first, I'm a cardboard cutout of myself, thinned by insecurity. But then I allow myself to lean into the music, however poorly played. And by leaning into the music, I find myself leaning into Johan, to this dance.

I look over his shoulder and see Ilsa extend a hand to Li, who takes it. Soon they're dancing, too. Then Parker, no doubt to annoy KK, asks Frederyk to dance, and Caspian, no doubt to annoy KK, accepts.

Jason isn't singing, so we all supply the words in our heads. This doesn't leave room for many other words, so instead of trying to speak, we rely on fingertips and motion, steps and sways.

It's not a long song, but when it's over and I check my watch, I see we've moved past midnight.

Johan says to me, "At the very least, we'll always have this."

And I think, yes, this is one of the fundamental things, too: Even in a world so full of conflict and panic and distraction and demand, two people can still find a peace like this, dancing to an old song. This is not hiding; this is finding. This is not retreat; it's a reminder of what matters.

Taxed by the demands of the keyboard, Jason steps away from the bench and moves to the record player. There, Ella Fitzgerald and Louis Armstrong have been waiting their turn. When the phonograph offers its arm, they take it and begin to sing about *the nearness of you.*

"This has been quite an evening," Johan says—and the way he says it makes it sound like it's coming to an end all too soon.

"I haven't shown you the roof yet," I offer.

"A wonderful point," he says. "I think it might be time for us to venture to the roof."

Parker and Frederyk join Jason by the record player, while KK pouts at her seat. All that's left on our makeshift dance floor is the nearness of Ilsa and Li. Johan and I leave them to it.

"We're going to the roof," I tell Parker. "Be back shortly."

Jason is displeased, but contains his displeasure. Caspian is encouraging, telling me to have fun.

"We'll hold down the fort," Parker promises.

I remember something and pick up a bag from the kitchen. Johan says he's not that hungry, but I tell him to wait. As we head upstairs, Ella and Louis fade behind us. The spirit of their song carries us along.

It should feel romantic. It should feel like we're coming up here to kiss, not sigh. But—

That's not what I'm feeling.

I'm feeling time going by.

I'm feeling I need to get to the fundamental truth of the night.

And while I like Johan, I don't think he's the truth I was supposed to find.

"It's a nice view," he says, and luckily, he's looking at the midnight skyline, not at me.

"It's not bad," I tell him. I take out two of the plastic bottles of bubble liquid that Jason brought as a host gift and give Johan one.

"Ah," he says approvingly.

We open the lids and retrieve our wands. It's strange to blow bubbles at night—they're barely there, but we know they're there.

I set the bubbles free over the streets of Manhattan. When I look over to Johan, I see that he isn't focusing on the bubbles—he's focusing on me.

There's such power in that. Being someone else's focus.

"Are you ready to leave it all behind?" he asks. He gestures to the city, which never recognizes such gestures.

I tell him, "I'm always jealous of people who get to be new to New York, because they get to be amazed by it in a way that I'll never be amazed by it. I know it's an extraordinary place, but it's always been ordinary to me, you know? And I worry that it's like living at a high elevation—I've gotten used to breathing here, and every part of my body is tuned to living here. I don't know anywhere else. I don't know how to live anywhere else. But I guess it's time for me to know somewhere else before this becomes the only place I ever know. There are all these kids who are struggling so hard to get to this city—I understand that so much. But I might need that in reverse."

"Why?" Johan asks, letting a parade of bubbles out in my direction. It's not a challenge; it's curiosity.

I catch one of the bubbles on my wand. "Our whole lives, Ilsa and I have been living this story. It's not a bad story. It's a good story. But—it's always the same story. And eighteen years old is way too young to have your story figured out. If you consider it written at eighteen, that means you haven't

been the one writing it—not that much of it, at least. I mean, look at you—you're, what, a nineteen-hour flight from home? You're living in a different part of the world and a different part of the day from all the people you grew up with."

"I left the nest," Johan says with a smile. There is one bubble still lingering between us.

"Yes—you left the nest. You might not have changed your character, but you definitely changed your story. And I—well, I need to do that, too. Don't you think?"

He tries to blow more bubbles, but the soap pops in the ring. He dips his wand again and this time puts the orbs into orbit.

"You owe it to yourself to try," he tells me. "And you may eventually owe it to yourself to fail. You'll see. It can be very lonely, and the second-guessing can be alarmingly severe. I love it here, but I still spend about half my waking thoughts on some variation of wondering whether I made the wrong choice. That's always going to be a part of it. But, like you said, I'd rather be exploring than be settled down at this point in my life. And there are so many things I've brought with me. My music. My studies. Dolly."

"Your homosexual flair," I say, sending some bubbles back his way. One of them catches in his hair before it disappears.

"Yes, my homosexual flair. Though I made sure to go somewhere that would give that flair enough oxygen to thrive."

"It's what Dolly would want."

"Certainly."

We're not touching, but it feels like we could at any moment.

I want to kiss you," I admit. "But I also don't want to kiss you, because I know that at some very definite point I would have to stop kissing you."

"I feel the exact same way. If you were staying, I would at the very least get another date out of you. But you're not staying. I think that much is clear. And I don't want to be a regret factor in that decision."

"Man," I say. "Aren't we mature?"

He laughs. "Absolutely." Then he leans in and kisses me. I kiss him back. Just once. It is definitely the first time I've ever kissed a boy with a bottle of bubble liquid in my hand.

"Okay, not *that* mature," he says. "I could've resisted doing that, but I didn't want to. Just one for the road."

"For new times' sake," I say.

"For new times' sake," he agrees.

Without thinking, I sigh. It's not a sigh of pleasure. And it's not a sigh of disappointment. It's just me taking in some of the air at this altitude, then letting it out again. One of those punctuation marks you deploy simply by being alive.

I turn to look at all the buildings around us. Johan stands so he can face them, too. There's something so invigorating about being surrounded by this many lights in the darkness, this many shapes for the eye to see. Intimidating, too. But mostly invigorating.

I have to imagine there will be something invigorating about being apart from them, too.

I imagine Czarina looking out the window of her Paris apartment, seeing a twist on this nightscape. Home but not quite. Similar street sounds, but a different underlying music.

And I imagine Ilsa still here. Ilsa without us. And it—

Well, it hurts to think of her like that.

Even if KK's here, too.

Especially if KK's here, too.

Johan's wand is out and he exhales bubbles into the night like Bogie once released cigarette smoke.

"Penny for your thoughts," he says.

"Just worried about my sister."

"I don't know either of you that well, but I sense—well, I sense that maybe the two of you need to have a talk? Your choice is going to be your choice—but let her into it, too. I made that mistake with some of my friends, and believe me, it's easier to let her in now than to try to get her back later."

"Good to know," I say. Then, feeling like I need to complete my doctorate in awkwardness, I add, "And it's good to know you, too."

"Likewise," he says. "And this isn't *it*, you know? We took a lot of subways in order to find each other—this is hardly the last stop."

I hug him then, and he hugs me back, and it could easily escalate from there, but it doesn't, because we are standing somewhere between the kiss and the sigh, and that is fundamentally okay.

"It's probably time for me to go home," he says, stealing one last glance at the city around us.

"And it's probably time for me and my sister to figure things out," I say. "Which will mean clearing out the guests."

"Good luck with that. I sense there's at least one guest she might not want to let go."

It makes me so happy that he's talking about Li here, not KK or even Parker.

"Before we go, there's one thing I've always wanted to do," he says. Then he explains. And there's no way I can object. For a frenzied minute, we are filling the air with as many bubbles as we can. And then, when we've achieved maximum bubblosity, we run through them, whooping all the way.

When that's done, we soapily small-talk our way down the stairs—conversing about the week ahead as if our weeks have long been familiar with one another. Ella and Louis are still singing when we get back to the apartment, although the record is on its other side now. In the dining room, Parker has broken out a broom and is sweeping up the glass and crumbs. Frederyk and Caspian are clearing the table. Nobody else is in evidence.

Seeing me notice, Parker explains, "Jason peaked fast, then fell hard. I tried to maneuver him back to your room, but he said he was scared to be here when Czarina learns you broke a glass—he nearly lost all his cookies when I told him what happened. So he's riding safely home as we speak. Li and Ilsa have taken themselves to Czarina's off-limits bedroom—but in the interest of full disclosure, I think it's for conversational privacy more than anything else. Sensing the wind-down, Freddie and I started to clean up. KK sat there for about a minute watching, then said we were too tedious to be bearable and retreated to her own apartment, where, of course, no such thing as cleaning up ever needs to happen. It is unclear whether she will be coming back or not."

"You don't need to clean," I tell him. I spot Johan starting to gather the coffee cups. "Seriously. I've got a system. You're doing me a favor by leaving it alone."

They all protest, and I counter-protest for about a minute, then Parker relents. I go to the lockbox and retrieve their phones—luckily, the combination has been changed to my dad's birthday, so I get it open on the fourth try.

"We're good here, then?" Parker asks as he and others pick up their phones. I take it as a compliment that nobody turns his on immediately.

I nod. "Yup. Go get some sleep."

"I'm holding you to California, man. I've already ordered a piano for my dorm room, so you're pretty much obligated."

I give him a hug. "It just may happen. We'll see."

"Meanwhile, tell your sister to unblock me, so I can thank her for the dance. And for not hating my guts anymore."

"Should I tell her that verbatim?"

"Maybe just the first part."

"Consider it done."

"I should probably take my leave as well," Caspian says. I am a little worried he, too, is going to want a hug, but instead he offers up Frederyk's pinkie again, and we shake. "I had no idea what to expect from this party, and I have to say, that was exactly what I got. Good luck with your journeying. If either of us can help in any way, let us know."

"Will do," I tell him.

"And thanks," Caspian adds. "For including us both."

"It was my pleasure," I say, looking Frederyk in the eye. Then I repeat it to Caspian, who nods.

Johan has retrieved his case and is clearly making to leave with the other three.

"You are an excellent recess from the humdrum," I tell him.

"And old flames can't hold a candle to you," he replies.

I'm sad to see him go—to see all of them go, really. But I also know the time has come to give the party its grace note and send it on its way.

When the door closes behind them, the apartment seems even emptier than it did before any of the guests arrived. I know there's still one around, but Czarina's bedroom is practically soundproofed. So I may as well be alone as I finish clearing the table, then push the coffee urn back into the kitchen to empty it in the sink. Everything I've done for the evening, I am now undoing. And the undoing, I find, is simply another form of doing.

I'm thinking about the future, but I don't want to think about it too much—not until I can talk to Ilsa about what we're going to do.

nineteen

ILSA

"Wake up, Ilsa."

I don't want to wake up. I'm having the sweetest dream about taking a bath in a tub filled with chocolate. The chocolate is creamy and heavenly until I turn on the shower spout. The spray of chocolate is indeed delicious, but really messy dripping from my hair, and practically blinds me. Like many of my ideas, the chocolate bath had seemed like a good one at the beginning, but as I step out of the tub, I wobble, and get chocolate all over the sink, floor, and wall. The bathroom is starting to look like a crime scene, from what I can glimpse through my chocolate-covered eyelashes. Is this what *death by chocolate* means?

I feel a hand running softly along my arm. No chocolate seems to be interfering with the hand's path. My eyes pop open. The dream is over. Another one is beginning.

"How long was I asleep?" I ask Li.

She's lying next to me, on her side, looking down at me. "Not long. Less than an hour."

I remember now. We came into Czarina's room to have some private time. To explore whether our lips wanted to explore more.

"Did I literally fall asleep on you?"

She laughs. "Pretty much. You drank too much. And you were over-stimulated."

Classic Ilsa. The life of the party who crashes hard just when things get interesting.

"Sorry," I say.

"There's nothing to apologize for. I had a little catnap, too. Snuggled against your cat dress."

"Are we already a lesbian stereotype? Should we just skip right to moving in together?"

"Hah!" The room is dark, but there is plenty of city light coming in through the window. I see Li smiling at me. "Did you know you sing in your sleep?"

"I do." My parents and Sam have been telling me this for years. I don't want to talk about this habit. I'm not embarrassed by it so much as worried that I reveal parts of myself I don't want revealed while I sleep. So I ask Li Zhang what I've wanted to know since our kiss on the rooftop. "How long have you liked me, Li?"

"I've always liked you."

"I mean, *like* like."

"I don't know. It just evolved. Sitting next to you in

chemistry every day, I noticed little things about you. Like how your backpack is always a mess but you have a plastic pencil case that you neatly put your pens and pencils into at the end of each class. That you quietly hum Beatles songs when you're working out chem problems. Like how you were always so patient with Igor Dimitrovich's stuttering when other kids teased, and always defended Jane Tomkins when the mean girls ganged up on her. How you called Mr. Abbott out on his patriarchal teaching methods and got the syllabus changed."

"Wow. I'm amazing," I joke.

Surprisingly, Li breaks out into song. *"The way you're singing in your sleep / The way you look before you leap / The strange illusions that you keep / You don't know / But I'm noticing."*

"That's really nice. Where'd you hear that?"

"I didn't. I saw it written on a bathroom wall at some music club down on the Lower East Side. It's kinda how I feel about you."

"I fear you might see a better version of me than I actually am," I confess.

"Then be that better version," she suggests.

Huh. There's something to that idea.

"Do you think I'm a bitch?" I ask.

"I think you have a bitchy sense of humor. That doesn't make you a bitch. But I like bitches, for the record. They get shit done." She reaches over to caress my hair. Then she presses her body closer to mine, leans down, and places her mouth on mine. This kiss is longer, and also a surprise—not for its sweetness (which is definitely there), but for its intensity.

It feels right.

I thought I wanted wild affairs. Really, what I want right now from Li is not the promise of a tempestuous dalliance. I want to share in Li's focus. And decency. The strength of her kiss that makes me want to be better than I am.

"I have to go home," Li says after our lips disengage.

"Stay over."

"My parents won't like that. My curfew is two a.m. If I take a ride service home now, I'll get there just in time."

"Were you serious about me coming to Taiwan with you?"

"Yes."

"Would that be weird? At your grandma's house, if we're . . . a couple?"

"We're not a couple. We're potential."

I'm not wounded at all by her statement. (If Parker had said it, I would have taken it as a failure on my part.) "Are you out to your family?"

"I'm neither in nor out even to myself. I don't believe in labels. Just in what feels right in my heart. I'm not positive that makes me gay. All I know is I'm not traditionally straight." She pauses, then says, "If you came with me to Taiwan, you'd sleep in the guest room, which is also my grandma's sewing room."

"No shenanigans," I tease.

"There might be shenanigans . . . eventually. I'm not in any rush. Are you?"

I don't even know what this is between us, other than I want to spend more time with her. Lots more. "No."

I've known Parker since he was in the same karate class with me and Sam when we were all eight years old. The moment I realized I liked him, when I was sixteen, was also the night we went all the way. I loved it. I loved him. But I wanted too much, too soon. I wasn't ready.

Next time, I want to be ready.

Li says, "I've never gone that far with anyone."

"Okay."

"Thank you."

"For what?"

"For not judging me about that. The few people I've told that to in the past made me feel like there was something wrong with me for being inexperienced in that way."

"There's nothing wrong with waiting."

I wish I'd waited.

Li says, "I agree! Whenever it happens, whoever it happens with, I want it to feel right."

"Kiss me?" I ask her. "As if it were the last time."

"I hope it won't be the last time!"

"The last time . . . tonight."

She complies.

It definitely won't be the last time.

I'm singing a tune as I find Sam in the kitchen cleaning up, after I return from downstairs and seeing Li get into her service car. *I don't want to leave her now / You know I believe and how.*

Sam, washing dishes in the sink, hands me a drying towel. I sit up on the counter next to him and start drying the pots in the rack. We always end parties here.

Sam says, "When you said you wanted a recess from the humdrum, I never imagined you meant Li Zhang!"

"I didn't, either. You know what, Sam?"

"What?"

"I *want* to be humdrum. Not boring, I guess—but consistent. You know?"

"A little bit of reckless is healthy. Please don't trade it all in for complete humdrum."

"Doubt that's possible." To prove it, I get off the counter and reach up to the cabinet with the last of Czarina's precious champagne flutes, retrieve one, and then take aim for the wall behind Sam. "Duck!" I warn him.

He begs, "No, Ilsa! Please don't do it! Czarina'll kill me if we lose one more of her glasses."

I put my hand down and return the flute safely to the cabinet. "Kidding."

"Not funny."

"Totally funny. What were you so worried about, anyway? You know she'll blame me."

"I'm sorry."

"That she'll blame me?"

"Yes. And for being the favorite."

It's taken eighteen years for him to specifically acknowledge this truth rather than deny it or pretend it's a joke.

The acknowledgment helps.

"It's okay," I say. "You'd be my favorite, too, if I was the grandma."

Sam waits, like I have more to say. I don't. Finally, he says, "Now's the time you're supposed to apologize for being Dad's favorite."

"I'm Dad's favorite?" It honestly never occurred to me. Parents of twins notoriously prioritize equality between siblings, so I never noticed a preference. "But you're the one who loves to cook and learned it from him."

"Dad loved cooking until he became a professional chef. Now it's a chore to him. You're the one who likes the stuff Dad likes. College basketball. Sudoku. *Seinfeld* reruns. Footlong subs." Sam shudders. "He appreciates you more because he gets you. I'm a mystery to him."

The only mystery to Dad about Sam, I think, is why Dad's own mother preferred her grandson to her son. Czarina appreciates Dad, most of the time. But she *adores* Sam, all of the time. Families are just like that, I guess. Maybe it doesn't have to mean they love each member any less.

"Do you really think Czarina has a secret lover?" I ask Sam.

"I honestly do. She wouldn't give up this apartment just for retirement."

"Maybe it's our grandfather she never acknowledges!" In Czarina's trail of broken hearts, the man who fathered our dad has always been the biggest mystery of all. She raised Dad on her own, and whatever happened between her and his father, no one knows, other than she went to work in

Paris for a summer, had a mad love affair, and returned home pregnant—and single.

"I know you want to be like Czarina," Sam says, sounding serious. "But in that way, please don't."

"I'll try. But you know I'm mean like her. How can I avoid it?"

"You're actually much nicer than her, when you're not trying to prove what a badass you think you have to be."

"You think I'm a badass?"

"Not at all. At heart, you're the biggest square of all of us."

I should be offended, but instead I laugh. "Does that make you the reckless one? Mister Going Off to California on a Whim?"

"Maybe."

"Good. It's the best thing that could ever happen to you."

"I thought you said you didn't believe I was capable of going."

"I was wrong." I was right that Sam needed a shock to his system to help him find his way. I was wrong that anybody but him could, or should, provide it. Is now the time to bring it up? Have Sam and I ever actually talked like this? For real, and not just for fun or show? "Wherever you go, I hope you find a place where you don't feel anxious and can just work on whatever you feel passionately about. Music. Cooking. Sock puppetry."

"Wherever you go, I hope it's not the Stanwyck. I think we all need to let go finally."

"I'm not going to live at the Stanwyck."

I don't know where I'm going to go. But I know I'm not going to stay here. Maybe that college thing my parents are so into is not a terrible idea. If I'm Dad's favorite, maybe he'll give me frequent-flyer miles to go to Taiwan this summer if I promise to go to Quinnipiac in the fall. And if I act like I really want to go to college. Maybe not even act. Maybe I'll legitimately be looking forward to it. The change of scenery. The new experience. The humdrum of Connecticut, within easy commute of Li Zhang, who starts at Queens College in the fall.

Sam says, "Czarina once told me she felt trapped by the Stanwyck. She wanted to go other places in her life but knew she'd never have a nicer place to live. What I think she wanted, secretly, was a *simpler* place to live. Where she didn't have to go to court against the building in order to stay in her own home. Or where she didn't have to hold on to the legend of her holding court over grand parties here."

"Sam?"

"Yes?"

"Do you love me more than Czarina?" I'm his twin. He *should*.

"I love you differently. No more, no less."

I go to the foyer to find my phone and return to the kitchen with it. I take the white chef's hat hanging on a hook and place it on Sam's head, and then I hold up the empty bottle of Czarina's best champagne. I hold out the phone to take a selfie to always remember our last dinner party at the Stanwyck. "Say, 'We'll always have Czarina's.'"

Sam smiles into the camera as I click the picture. "We'll always have Czarina's."

Then he takes the bottle from my hand and pours the last remaining drops over my head, like a most excellent baptism into our unknown future, where anything can happen and hopefully it won't suck but will involve great food, good times, the occasional sock puppet, and the people we love the most.

"Cheers," I tell my brother.

Sam picks up a Dolly figurine from the counter. Johan must have left it behind. I wonder why.

Apparently it's because Dolly has something to say.

twenty

SAM

I'm guessing the message is this:

If diminutive, spirited Dolly can arm-wrestle a big bro like Sylvester Stallone into submission, then I can take control of my own life.

twenty-one

SAM&ILSA

Ten Years Later

They don't recognize the girl who answers the door, and she doesn't recognize them, either. Not at first.

It takes Ilsa a second. Then she figures it out: This young woman in front of them has to be—

"Maddy?"

The girl—she must be eighteen now, Ilsa realizes—doesn't look any less confused.

"Maddy, it's me, Ilsa. And this is Sam. We were up at KK's and decided to come down here. To see the apartment again."

"Ilsa! Wow!" Maddy wraps her in a hug. Then she stands back and takes in what Ilsa and Sam are wearing. "Of course—your grandmother! I was so sorry to hear the news. Did you just come from . . . ?"

"The funeral. Yes," Sam says. He is trying very hard to reconcile the teenager in front of him with the little girl who used to live next door. Even though they've visited KK a few times in the intervening years, this is the first time they've been on this floor since Czarina moved out.

"Can we come in?" Ilsa asks. "Just to see it."

"Of course!" Maddy says. "Mom and Dad aren't home, just me. They'll be so sad they missed you. Come in!"

Maddy opens the door, heads back inside, and has no idea how strange it is for them to be beckoned through their own doorway. Ilsa follows, then notices Sam's hesitation, recognizes his fear and his sadness. They are walking into the past, and it's not going to be the same as it was.

Without a word, she takes his hand. Without a word, he lets her. Together, they step inside.

Sam doesn't want to look around, but he can't help it. It's like seeing a familiar person in completely different clothes. Or maybe it's like seeing familiar clothes on a completely different person. Some of Czarina's furniture remains—there was no point, she said, in carrying a sofa all the way to Paris, and it chilled her to think of anything she loved in a storage unit. Maddy's family was happy to accept the leftovers, and as a result, Sam feels both at home and completely out of context.

Ilsa isn't looking at the apartment as much as she's looking at Maddy. She can't believe how old Maddy is. And at the same time, she can't believe how young Maddy is, because isn't she the same age Ilsa and Sam were when they were throwing dinner parties here? Hadn't being a senior in high school seemed so *old* at the time? And wasn't eighteen, really, when you got into the wider, later world, so much younger than you once thought it was?

"I'm sorry it's such a mess," Maddy is saying now. "If I'd known you were coming by, I would have cleaned up a little bit. I mean, it must be weird, right? To see it like this?" She gathers a magazine from the couch, as if that is enough to mark an improvement. "God, I remember coming in here when I was little—you guys were *so loud*. And my bedroom was *right there*." She points to one of the living room walls. "Before we connected everything, my bed was right up against that wall. I remember lying there and listening to you. It was loud, but it always sounded . . . happy. I tried to find any excuse to come over. Just to see what you were doing."

"You brought us cookies," Sam says, a vague memory returning to him.

"I think I did! Wow. And your grandmother—she was something else."

Sam smiles. "Yeah, she really was."

She hadn't wanted to be buried in Paris. She'd loved it there, but this was home.

Ilsa can see the slipping of her brother's smile, the effort to hold it all together when really some of it had to be let go. It had been her idea to come here, and now she wonders whether it was a good idea. Well, good or bad, it needed to happen. Sam had spent the past few months in Paris, had been with Czarina to the end, just as she'd wanted. He had been so strong for their grandmother, for all of them. But now, Ilsa saw, he had no idea what to do with the rest of that strength. She didn't want him converting it into sadness. She wanted to remind him of what he had set out to do.

"Would you mind giving us a few minutes?" Ilsa asks Maddy now. "Then the three of us can catch up—it's been so long!"

"Sure. Of course," Maddy says. "And I can't wait to catch up, either. Just don't ask me where I'm going to school. I'm sick of people asking where I'm going to school!"

"It's a deal," Ilsa says.

Maddy points in the direction of Czarina's old bedroom. "I'll be in my room if you need me. Just call when you're ready."

She leaves, and Ilsa and Sam are once more in their universe of two. The whole weekend, they've retreated into it when the social obligations have been too overwhelming.

"I wonder where she's going to school," Sam says.

"You're awful," Ilsa tells him, in the tone reserved for people who are never awful.

Ilsa hears footsteps through the ceiling, and even though she knows KK and Li are a few floors above, she likes to think it's them, anyway. Being in KK's apartment was the antithesis of being in this one—even though it was full of plenty of new things, it felt like it hadn't changed at all. KK, however, had—or maybe it was just Czarina's death that made her a little less sure of herself, and thus a little more ready to listen to others. "I thought she'd live forever," she'd whispered to Ilsa during the funeral. "I always wanted to be just like her. Now I don't know who to be."

Li, sitting between KK and Ilsa, had squeezed Ilsa's hand, there for her as always, the constant support on which a new life had been built.

And on Ilsa's other side: Sam. After ten years of traveling and teaching and touring, he'd returned to New York. The city he had to leave, but which had never left him.

We should go to the kitchen, Ilsa thinks, at the same time that Sam says, "Let's check out the kitchen."

They're still like that. Even now. Whether they go three hours or three weeks or three months between conversations, when they do talk, their thoughts and words share the same space.

The kitchen is almost exactly the same. Czarina had been so proud of it, had invested so much in it. It makes sense that there hasn't been much room for improvement since.

Sam runs his hand over the counter, and as he does, it's as if his eighteen-year-old self is beside him, doing the same thing. And if his eighteen-year-old self is beside him, that means that Ilsa's eighteen-year-old self is also in the room.

Sam thinks, *You leave the place you're from. You have to. But you also need to have it stay in you for a long time. It is your center.*

And then he looks at Ilsa. Ilsa, now. His other center.

"Remember that night?" he says. He doesn't have to say which night. He still has Dolly in his pocket. She's been his talisman.

"The night we promised," she says. "The night we said goodbye."

It hadn't been their last night in the apartment—there were many other nights there, packing up, preparing Czarina for her emigration. But Sam thinks Ilsa is exactly right—the night of the party was indeed the night they said goodbye to the lives they'd had . . . and hello to what their lives would become.

"I have to take a picture for Parker," Sam says. Parker had wanted to fly in for the funeral, but Gina would have killed him a thousand different ways if she'd gone into labor while he was across the country; Parker had agreed the timing was not ideal, and had stayed home to await the imminent arrival of his first daughter.

Ilsa doesn't expect to be in the picture, but when she sees Sam is pointing the phone in her direction, she strikes a merengue pose. Sam laughs, which is wonderful to hear.

"Well done," he says, sending the photo on its way.

There are some things about high school that Sam has completely forgotten, like #Stantastic's tweets or Trader Joe's Boy or anything having to do with calculus. But he remembers that night clearly. And their conversation at the end of it.

"Promise me you won't stay here," he'd asked.

"I promise," she'd said. "If you promise me you'll leave, too."

And he'd promised as well.

That could have been it. They'd never made promises like this before. They'd asked each other things, sure. They'd made each other swear on the truth, or swear to secrecy. But not promises. Not with the stakes so high and the determination so important. They hadn't made promises to each other

207

because they both knew that to make the promises meant that they needed to be kept. No matter what.

Once they started, they couldn't stop.

"Promise me you'll tell me if you need help," she said.

He promised.

"Promise me you'll find things to love," he said.

She promised, thinking of Li.

"Promise me you'll make music," she said.

He promised, thinking of Johan.

"Promise me that wherever you go, you'll learn how to do your own laundry," he said.

She promised.

This was their secret, now exposed: The things they wouldn't do for themselves, they would do for each other. They had known this all along.

And this was, in fact, how it had worked out. Sam had seen the world, and Ilsa had seen the workings of her own heart. Sam had held his music without choking it, and Ilsa had learned a way to not only find fault, but fix some of the faults she found. They both found happiness by understanding there were going to be many times when they were not happy. They both found strength in discovering happiness could be found outside of them as well as within.

The ending, it appeared, had indeed been a beginning.

Now, another ending. Czarina gone, but the two of them still here. And this kitchen . . . still here.

"Remember the time . . . ," Ilsa begins.

The conversation that follows lasts for over four hours.

Eventually Maddy comes back and joins them, and KK and Li come down and join in as well. They talk and remember, remember and talk. Even the humdrum seems magical, when seen from afar.

In their way, they bring it all back to life.

ACKNOWLEDGMENTS

Thank you to Nancy Hinkel, who is always the life of our party.

Thank you to Stephen Brown, Jenny Brown, and even people whose last names are not Brown at Random House Children's Books. We raise a toast to you.

Thank you to Jennifer Rudolph Walsh and Alicia Gordon and everyone else we work with at WME, and to Bill Clegg and everyone at the Clegg Agency. You are all masters of seating arrangements.

Thank you to Stella Paskins and everyone at Egmont UK, to Susannah Chambers and everyone at Allen & Unwin in Australia, and to our other foreign publishers, who make the party global.

Thank you, as always, to our family and friends, with the assurance that dinner parties with you usually go better than the one depicted in this novel. Usually.

And thank you to our readers. You're the reason we threw this party in the first place.